J
FICTION
LACHTMAN

Lachtman, Ofelia
  Dumas.

Call me Consuelo.

Call Me
Consuelo

by

Ofelia Dumas Lachtman

Arte Público Press
Houston, Texas
1997

This volume is made possible through grants from the National Endowment for the Arts (a federal agency), Andrew W. Mellon Foundation, the Lila Wallace-Reader's Digest Fund and the City of Houston through The Cultural Arts Council of Houston, Harris County.

Recovering the past, creating the future

Arte Público Press
University of Houston
Houston, Texas 77204-2090

Interior illustration by Virginia Roeder
Cover design by Gladys Ramirez
Cover illustration by Daniel Lechón

Lachtman, Ofelia, Dumas.
　　Call me Consuelo / by Ofelia Dumas Lachtman.
　　　　p.　　cm.
　　Summary: After suddenly being orphaned, twelve-year-old Consuelo reluctantly moves in with her American grandmother while hoping to return soon to her Mexican American family.
　　ISBN 1-55885-187-9 (paper : alk. paper).
　　— ISBN 1-5585-188-7 (clothbound : alk. paper)
　　[1. Moving, Household—Fiction. 2. Grandmothers—Fiction. 3. Mexican Americans—Fiction.] I. Title.
　　PZ7.L13535Cal　1997
　　[Fic]—dc21　　　　　　　　　　　　　96-50201
　　　　　　　　　　　　　　　　　　　　CIP
　　　　　　　　　　　　　　　　　　　　AC

The paper used in this publication meets the requirements of the American National Standard for Permanence of Paper for Printed Library Materials Z39.48-1984. ∞

Call Me Consuelo

Chapter One

I pressed my face close to the airplane's little window and looked down at the city of Los Angeles. The brown hills and buildings got blurry and swimmy and I blinked my eyes fast. I didn't want my grandmother, who was sitting right next to me, to see me cry. I put my hand against my chest. Right through my T-shirt I could feel the silver locket I was wearing. It always made me feel better to know it was there, especially now.

The airplane got closer and closer to the ground. Everything looked hot and dry. Back home in Dos Palos it was already getting colder and the trees were turning gold.

❧❧❧

The only trees I saw here were a few palms, tall and skinny, and dusty green. Pretty soon we were swooping down right over the airport. There was a soft bump as the plane touched land and then it raced along the runway.

Later, after my grandmother and I picked up our suitcases, we dragged them out of the huge airport building and stopped by the automatic doors. "Be a good girl, Connie," she said. "Stand right here with our bags while I find a taxi."

I watched her step out to the curb. Her name is Grace Harburton. She's my grandmother on my father's side, and she likes me to call her Grace. I don't like to be called Connie. My name isn't Connie. It's María Consuelo Harburton, and my mother and father always called me Consuelo. My father said he loved my name because it meant "comfort" in Spanish, and that's what I was to him—except, he would add, when I got pigheaded about something.

Before we left Dos Palos—for the three whole days that Grace was there—I didn't say anything about her calling me Connie. I don't know why... except that I didn't want to explain how I felt about everything: I was leaving my Tía Alma and Tío Fernando and all my cousins to go to Los Angeles to live with her.

I told myself that it wasn't fair. But deep down I knew it really was. Two years ago, when my mother and father were killed in a car accident, the judge said Grace was my legal guardian. That time I put up such a holler at having to leave Dos Palos that Grace said, "Okay, honey. Since your Aunt Alma says it's all right, you can stay here, at least for a while."

I stayed for over a year and a half. Tía Alma and Tío Fernando were second best to having my own folks. After all, I've known them since the day I was born. I secretly planned to live with them always. But it didn't work out that way. When Tío Fernando lost his job in the mine, Grace came to get me. They didn't want me to leave, but Grace insisted. I belonged with her, she said. Tears come almost every time I think about that. My cousin Rebecca says I'm too old to cry. Maybe she's right. I'm going to be twelve in December, and that's only three months away.

Grace showed up just then, pointing to a yellow taxi. "We'll soon be home," she said as we climbed into the back seat. But we drove through streets so jammed with cars and people that it made me feel a million miles from home. Dos Palos is a mining town up in the mountains of Central California that has only one stop signal. So you know it doesn't have a lot of cars.

"Where are they all going?" I asked.

Grace shrugged. We drove by a few tall buildings, and I twisted my neck to look at them. Grace said, "Later, when we're all settled in, there'll be a lot of interesting things for you to see."

"I guess," I said, and sat back. What I really wanted to see was the brook that runs behind my aunt's house. Or maybe the pond, where we all swim and climb trees.

Before I knew it, we had come to a sign that said Shadywood Knolls. It was a big place, with a high brick fence all around it. We turned into a street called Woodside Lane. But we didn't get far. There were wooden arms, like those at a train crossing, stopping us. They were by a guardhouse right in the middle of the street.

The guard, a skinny old man with crooked gold-rimmed glasses, stuck his head out. "Hello, Mrs. Harburton," he said. "Good thing you're back. Things are in a mess. Juan Pablo is missing."

"Missing? What do you mean?"

"He hasn't shown up for three days."

"Three days?" Grace said. "Why, he was here Thursday morning when I left for Dos Palos."

"He was here Thursday morning, all right," the gateman said, "but not since then."

"Oh, my," Grace said. "We'll have to do something about that."

The old man nodded. "I hope so." He pushed a button in a panel in front of him. Up went the wooden arm and in we went.

I wanted to ask who Juan Pablo was and could he speak Spanish, because I'd need *someone* to talk Spanish with. My mother would want me to; she'd even taught my father. But I could see that Grace had other things on her mind, so I thought I'd better wait.

Woodside Lane wound in and around a lot of two-story buildings. There were trees and other green things growing around them. I thought I saw a little red bridge in between a couple of trees. If there was a bridge, there was bound to be water, at least a little stream. I know I saw a boy sitting on an upstairs balcony flying paper planes. One flew down and hit the side of the taxi. Poking up behind the roof of the house where the boy was sitting was an old wooden tower. I swung around to get a good look at it. It was made of old logs, like a tower in a fort. There was even a flag, a ragged red flag. Weird. What was it doing here?

The taxi made another turn and stopped in front of a building with two doors marked 172A and 172B. Grace said, "Well, here we are. That wasn't far," and patted my knee.

We all got out. The driver went around to the trunk of the car. Grace went up the steps to the door of 172B. I went to follow her, but stopped on the bottom step. Someone was shouting down at us.

"Hey, Mrs. Harburton, you're back!" A freckled face with short red hair around it poked out from an upstairs window. "It's about time, too! I was sure you'd gotten lost, or something. Boy! Tag sure missed you."

"I missed him, too," Grace called.

I said, "Who's that?"

"Tag? Tag's my dog. His name's Tagalong."

"No, not Tag. The redhead."

"Oh, that's Queen Isabella." Grace called up to the open window, "Your majesty, this is my granddaughter, Connie."

I can't explain why, but I saw red. And not on anyone's head either. "No, I'm not!" I shouted to the girl above. My name's María Consuelo Harburton. And please call me Consuelo!"

Chapter Two

My grandmother's face looked peculiar as we walked into the house. It was kind of pinched together, the way my little cousin Fernando's looked whenever he was hurt and about to cry. But I couldn't imagine Grace crying. Anyway, what was there to cry about?

She closed the door. We were in a hallway with stairs facing the front door. To the right of the stairs was a large room with couches and chairs and a lot of bright cushions. On the other side there was a room with a table and chairs that I figured was a dining room.

❧❧❧

Grace sighed and said, "I'm sorry, honey. I wish you'd told me before how you felt about being called Connie. Consuelo is a lovely name, and that's what I'll be sure to call you. All right?"

"All right," I said. The words came out sounding more like, "Ahrawrrr," because I had trouble pushing them by a lump that had jumped into my throat.

"Well, then," my grandmother said, "let's leave our suitcases right where they are and go up and see your room."

If the room she led me to had been in Dos Palos, I guess I would have loved it. But I was pretty sure I would never love anything in Los Angeles. Still, it was awfully pretty. It had pale green and yellow flowered curtains. And the same flowers were on the bedcover and cushions. And sitting on top of a small chest of drawers was a TV. A TV! All to myself. I bit my lip. I wasn't sure watching TV all by myself was going to be that much fun. Standing there in the middle of that pretty room with Grace opening windows and closet doors, my eyes got wet and I started blinking again. I had to stop feeling sorry for myself. As soon as Tío Fernando finds a job, I thought, I'm somehow going to fix it to go back home to live.

Grace asked if I wanted help bringing up my suitcases.

"No, thank you," I said, and ran down the stairs for them. By the time I dragged them both up the stairs, my eyes were dry and she had disappeared. So I went downstairs again and brought her suitcase up, too.

In a few minutes I heard the front door open and close and Grace talking to someone.

"I'm glad to hear you behaved," she was saying. And then, "All right, all right, go see for yourself. She's a very nice girl. You're going to like her."

The next thing I heard was a scurrying sound on the stairs and a sort-of-gray, sort-of-brown, kind-of-dirty-white short-legged little dog racing into my bedroom. I was standing by an open dresser drawer with a pair of socks in my hand, but I tossed them back into the suitcase and picked up the little dog.

❧❧❧

"Oh, Tag," I said, "I'm glad to meet you." And I really was. He wriggled in my arms, then licked my cheek, so I guess he was glad to meet me, too. When I put him down, he sniffed in my suitcases and found one of my sandals to chew on. I took it away from him and put him on a cushion on the floor where he right away fell asleep.

That night my grandmother and I ate in the kitchen.

Grace smiled and said, "I hope you don't mind eating in the kitchen."

I shook my head. "That's where we always ate. I like kitchens." But what a difference. Of course, I didn't say that. Tía's kitchen back home in Dos Palos is bigger than my new bedroom. It has a big table in the middle of it that always has a basket of fruit on it. There's stuff all over the refrigerator that the eight-year-old twins, Fernando and Felicia, have made. And photographs. Even one of my mother and father. Tía made me take that one with me. She said my grandmother Grace would want it on her refrigerator if she didn't already have one. But there was nothing on Grace's refrigerator, except a little bowl of artificial flowers on top.

At bedtime, Grace came in and said good night and said she hoped I wasn't too lonely.

"I'm all right," I said.

"Sure?"

I nodded.

She looked at me with a sad little smile. "Well, good night then." She closed the door softly.

When she was gone I opened up the locket I always wear around my neck. It opens on a little hinge and has a picture of my mother on one side and my father on the other. I looked at them for a moment, whispered good night like I always do, and turned off the light.

Of course I was lonely. For the last couple of years I had shared a bedroom with my cousins, Rebecca and Monica. Before that, I had a little room right next to my folks' bedroom, and my cat, *Guapo*, nearly always slept with me. *Guapo* means handsome in Spanish, and my father, who was kind of funny that way, named our cat that because he said he was so ugly. He really wasn't.

Just kind of long and skinny. I had to give him away when I went to live with my aunt's family because the twins are allergic to cats.

But all this remembering wasn't making me any less lonely. So I got up and looked out the window. Across the wall, in someone else's yard, I heard somebody laughing, and that made me even more lonely. So I got back in bed.

I heard my grandmother moving around in her bedroom and the water running in her bathroom. That made me feel a *little* better. It was good to know there was *some-one* close by. Then I heard another sound. A small scratchy sound that was kind of scary until I heard the whine.

I jumped out of bed and opened my door. Tag leaped into the room. He raced past me, his short little legs going a mile a minute, and somehow—I'll never know how—bounded up onto the bed. There he lay panting, his bright eyes daring me to put him on the floor. But that was the last thing I was going to do. I crawled under the blankets, and, little by little, Tag snuggled up against me.

I fell asleep wondering about two things. What was the weird tower with the faded red flag doing in this fancy neighborhood? And how did Tag get over the wire-mesh fence that Grace kept between the kitchen and the rest of the house?

Chapter Three

The next day was Sunday. After break-
fast Grace said, "I'm sorry, honey, but I have
to work at my computer for a couple of hours
this morning. I'm really behind in my work.
If you'll be patient, maybe this afternoon we
can go to a movie."

"That's okay," I said, but I wasn't sure it
was. At home we all got dressed up and went
to church—and *then* a movie. To go to
church we had to drive to Redtree, a town
fifteen miles away from Dos Palos, but
nobody complained. After church and before
the movie we had *menudo*. In Redtree
there's a restaurant called La Olla that
makes the best *menudo*. *Menudo* is a soup

made with little squares of meat from the inside of the cow and lots of puffed-up white corn and chili and tons of cilantro and other good things. Even my father, who wasn't Mexican, really loved it.

Grace was still talking. "While you wait for me, why don't you look around Shady-wood? The swimming pool's two short blocks behind us. There are a number of children who live in Shadywood. I'll bet they'll be at the pool."

I nodded. I guess that was something to do. I'd already made my bed. Grace says keeping my room picked up is the only chore I have.

"Just don't go beyond the fence," Grace added. "Not until I show you how to get back in."

"Are we locked in here or something?" I asked.

"No, no. The gates are for our protection."

"From what?"

"From... from... oh, people who shouldn't be in here."

That wasn't a very good explanation, but I didn't care. I wasn't going toward the gate.

Nor the swimming pool. I was going to look for the tower.

Outside, I ran into the redhead from 172A. She was in a bathing suit, with a towel over her arm. She looked as thin as a river reed, with freckles and carrot-red hair that's short and bristly as a scrub brush.

"Hi," she said, "I'm..."

"I know. You're Queen Isabella."

"Not really. That's just what Mrs. Harburton calls me. My name's Isabel Queen, and I'm eight years old. What's your real name?"

"Consuelo."

"Consuelo," Isabel said with a frown on her face. "Okay. You'd better call me Queenie." With that, she turned around, raced along the path and disappeared.

I walked toward where I'd seen the tower. For a while I walked behind a man and woman who were talking about Juan Pablo. But all I heard beside his name was that "it was disgraceful" and that "something should be done about it."

After a little bit I came upon the red bridge. And there *is* water. A little brook that wanders around the buildings and ends in a small round pool. The pool has some pretty gold and red fish in it, but I didn't stay there too long. I wanted to see the tower. I finally did. It was on the other side of a high brick fence at the back end of Shadywood.

I walked along the fence. The closer the tower got, the higher the fence seemed to be. I was ready to give up when I saw the tree. It was a tall, skinny tree that looked as if it wanted to grow big, but somebody kept cutting it back. Kind of like Queenie's hair. Even so, it was a good climbing tree. Rebecca had taught me how to pick out the good ones. This one looked like a rubbery kind of tree, one that would bend before it broke, and it had a fork low enough to reach.

I was wearing jeans and sneakers. Good thing. There's nothing better for climbing. So up I went. The trunk was smooth, and even though the bark scraped off easily, I made it to the fork on my second try. When I saw what was on the other side of the fence, I almost fell out of the tree.

The fort, and it *was* a fort: log walls and all. It was in a straight line from the tree, about half a block away. A fort! Why? And why all the other stuff?

Across from the fort there was an old-time street. It was made up mostly of two-story buildings with a narrow wooden sidewalk running in front of them. The buildings looked like shops. I swear that on the window of one was printed, "New York Gazette," but I really had to squint to see that.

Way in the back, against a board fence that surrounded everything, was a big building with rounded towers and turrets. A castle. It had to be a castle. I was *sure* it was a castle. But I wanted to get a better look. I climbed up higher in the tree. I was holding on to a small branch when I heard the shout.

"Hey!"

I let go of the little branch and it swung back and hit me. I hung on for dear life. When the tree and I had stopped shaking, I squirmed around to see who was yelling at me. There was nobody on the ground.

"Hey, you!" The shout came again. "Get out of that tree!"

The yells came from the building just behind me. Somebody pounded at a window that was higher than my head. I looked up and saw a round, pushed-in face pressed against the glass. Ugly. And scary, too. Quickly, I shimmied down the tree and, without even a backward look, raced toward the red bridge.

I couldn't wait to ask my grandmother about the things I'd seen. When I ran into the house, I shouted, "Grace! Grace, where are you?"

Grace appeared at the top of the stairs. "Consuelo, what is it? Is something wrong?"

"Oh, no. It's just that I saw the fort and I..." I stopped.

My grandmother was looking down at me and laughing. She sat down on the top step and said, "So you discovered the old movie lot, did you?"

And that's how I learned that Shadywood Knolls is built on the grounds of an old movie studio and that what I had seen was the remaining back lot.

Grace went on to tell me that the fort, the castle and the old-time street had appeared in lots of movies and television shows. "It's all going to be torn down soon," she said, "to make room for a new section of Shadywood Knolls."

Right then and there I decided what I had to do. And soon. Explore the back lot. No matter who, or what, yelled at me.

Chapter Four

Of course I had forgotten about school. That I'd have to go to school, that is, and not spend the next day looking around the movie lot. But at bedtime Grace reminded me.

"Franklin Middle School is only three short blocks from here," she said. "So you'll be able to walk there. Isn't that lucky?"

I nodded, thinking that I'd never walked to school before. A bus had picked me up ever since I'd first started. "Who's the sixth-grade teacher?" I asked.

Grace looked puzzled for a moment, then said, "The way the schools are here, you'll have a home room teacher for announcements and such and then five or six others for your subjects."

Now it was my turn to look puzzled. I know I was frowning because Grace patted my arm and said, "It'll all fall into place once you're there. You'll see."

I knew what she was talking about. There'd been TV shows about schools in big cities like New York and Beverly Hills where the kids all hustled through crowded halls each time a bell rang. "I guess so," I said. "I just didn't know sixth grade was like being in high school."

Grace smiled and said good night. And then I lay in my bed wondering how it would be to go to a school where I didn't know anybody. Back in Dos Palos I'd known not just the kids, but most of their families, too. Well, I'd soon find out. I punched the pillow and flopped over on my stomach. I was kind of glad Grace was going with me the next day.

When we started out in the morning, we didn't go by the guardhouse. We went out through a walk-in gate. It was at the opposite end of Shadywood and you had to have a key to open it. Grace used hers this time, but she gave me one to put on the ring with my house key.

The first bell was ringing when we reached Franklin School. It was a long, low building, cream colored with green around the windows and on the doors. Kids, mostly in shorts even though it was late in September, rushed over the bright green grass and through the big double doors. I was glad I'd worn shorts, too.

It took a long time to get me registered. When we were done Grace said, "Good-bye then, honey. I'll wait for you right here after your last class."

A couple of boys sitting on a bench near the office door snickered, and I know my face turned red.

"I can find my own way back, thank you."

Grace threw me a surprised look. "Sure?"

I nodded, one quick nod.

"Okay, then," she said. "I have a house I can show this afternoon. I'll go ahead and do that." Grace sells houses, and I guess she was pretty busy. She was probably glad she didn't have to come get me.

"Okay," I said. "See you."

The second-period class was English. The office secretary took me there. After looking at my papers, the teacher pointed out an empty place and said, "Sit there." I don't think she liked to be interrupted.

My seat was a couple of rows behind a girl with long blonde hair. I noticed her because she kept tossing her head and swinging her hair over her shoulder. Her hair was straight and shiny, and it always fell smoothly down her back. Just like a TV ad. My hair is black and curly—and short. It's easier that way.

When the bell rang, I went into the hall with all the other kids. But I didn't keep going. I had to figure out how to find Room 115. I didn't figure long. Somebody tapped my shoulder and said, "Hi."

It was the blonde girl from English. She swung her hair over her shoulder again. "My name's Lish," she said. "Alicia really. What's yours?"

"Consuelo. Just Consuelo."

❧❦❧

"Well, where are you going next?"

"Art," I said, "if I can find the room."

"No problem. That's where I'm going. Come on."

Lish was the only one I met who was really friendly. I tried to find her at lunchtime and didn't. But I *did* find the cafeteria.

I guess school cafeterias are all alike. Kind of steamy, with beaten-up tables and chairs and crowded bulletin boards. They even smell the same. No wonder. As I moved my tray along the food line, I saw that they had cheese enchiladas that were all smothered with tomato sauce. I knew just what they would taste like. So I had a bowl of chili beans. Anyway, I was kind of hungry for beans. We had refried beans at every meal at home.

I headed for an empty table in a corner next to a bunch of noisy kids. Even before I sat down I knew that they were talking Spanish. A girl with black hair as short as mine and mile-long lashes kept staring at me, so I smiled. She didn't smile back.

Instead she frowned and nudged a boy sitting by her.

"What's she doing in our corner?" she asked in Spanish.

The boy shrugged, then grinned. "Wait till Juan and Gato find that their table's taken," he said in Spanish. "Wheeuw!"

I can take a hint, in Spanish or in English, so I got up and picked up my tray. Then they really stared. I found another table that was only half full and ate my chili beans silently.

Lish wasn't in any of my other classes. Not even home room.

Just before the last bell rang, Mrs. Kessler, the home room teacher, asked, "Is there anyone here from Shadywood Knolls?"

I looked around and, when nobody said anything, I raised my hand, but not too high.

Mrs. Kessler said, "You're the new girl, aren't you?"

I thought that was a pretty dumb thing to ask, so I didn't say yes or no. I said, "I'm Consuelo."

ՁԺՆՁ

"Well, Consuelo, will you please take these papers to Russell Neeland? He lives in Shadywood and he's stuck at home. I know he'll appreciate it."

I took the papers. What else could I do?

The three blocks home were easy. There was just one traffic signal to cross, and what was new about that? We have a signal light in Dos Palos, too. I had to admit, though, that I was glad to see the black iron gate to Shadywood. Then all I had to do was find Blue Stone Road and deliver that boy's papers.

I dug in my pocket for my keys, put the gate key in the lock and turned it. Or tried to. The key wouldn't turn. I pulled it out and started all over again. I tried one way, then the other. Nothing worked. I was getting pretty mad. When I finally gave up, I took being mad out on the gate. I grabbed the bars and shook them. "Dumb old lock!" I grumbled. I was about to give the gate a good, solid kick when I felt a heavy hand on my shoulder.

I swung around fast. A man with a big flabby belly was standing right next to me.

"Leave me alone!" I said. "My father told me about men like you."

The man opened his mouth to say something, but I didn't give him a chance. "If you don't go away I'll yell for the police!"

"That suits me fine," the fat man growled. "Then you can explain to them what you're doing to that gate."

"I don't talk to strangers," I said, and whirled around. I started to run, but I was yanked back. The awful man had grabbed my book bag.

"Stoppit! You're hurting me!" I shouted.

"You're going in the wrong direction," the man said. "We're sick and tired of you Arroyo Street kids breaking into our project." He gave me a little shove. "Go on back where you belong!"

I'm usually a pretty good talker, but that really got to me. All I did was stare at him. I don't know what I would have done next if I hadn't heard a voice I recognized.

"Hi, Mr. Crane. Hi, Consuelo. What's up?" It was Lish, her blonde hair gleaming in the sunlight.

"You know this girl, Alicia?"

❧❧❧

"Sure. She's from my school. What's wrong?"

I shook my head. "Nothing's wrong," I muttered, "except him."

"Sure I know her," Lish said. "She's waiting for me. We're going to my house." Lish put a key in the lock and turned it. The gate opened easily.

We stepped inside and I looked at Lish with her blue, blue eyes and glimmering hair. I swear right then I loved her.

"Well, in that case," the ugly man called Crane said, "just tell her not to tear the place down next time."

Once on the other side of the gate, I became very brave. "And tell *him* to keep his hands to himself. That's... that's... child abuse."

Lish looked at me and giggled, and then I was giggling, too.

We watched Mr. Crane get into a car at the curb and drive away. Lish said, "What *were* you doing at the gate?"

"Trying to get in."

"Oh." Lish's face got serious. "You're not supposed to. Only people with keys. People who live here."

❧❦❧

"I live here," I said, and pulled out my key ring. "I live with my grandmother on Woodside Lane. And I have a key. But it won't work."

"You do? You have? Those stupid keys. I couldn't work mine at first either. Let's try yours again."

Of course, it worked for Lish. I might have known. But after a few tries the key turned in the lock for me, too. I thanked Lish for rescuing me from Mr. Ugly Crane and for helping me with the key. Then I said, "I've got to find Blue Stone Road."

"Thought you lived on Woodside," Lish said.

"I live on Woodside, all right," I said in a cold voice, "but I have some papers from school for a boy on Blue Stone. So I'd better get going."

"For Rusty Neeland, I'll bet," Lish said, tossing her hair over her shoulder. She bit her lip and shrugged a little. I could tell she was uncomfortable. "Yuck!" she said. "I guess I sounded like fat Mr. Crane. I'm sorry. Don't be mad at me."

Chapter Five

"I'm not mad," I said, and I started walking. And I wasn't. After all, Lish had rescued me from that fat man. I wasn't ever going to forget that. "Why did he call me an 'Arroyo Street kid?'" I asked.

Lish shrugged. Her face turned from creamy to a pale, pale pink, like the color of big white clouds at sunset. "He doesn't know what he's talking about," she said. "He thought you came from Arroyo Street. He thought you were Mexican."

"I am," I said with a firm nod. "And American, too. Where's Arroyo Street?"

◈◈◈◈

"Four or five blocks from here. In a little ravine in the hills on the other side of the movie lot."

"What's wrong with the kids there?"

"Nothing. Mr. Crane hates everybody, especially kids... and they hate him."

"I don't blame them."

She tugged at my arm. "If you're going to Rusty's, you'd better turn this way. Mind if I go with you?"

I said no, and we didn't say anything more until we got to Blue Stone Road.

Then, in the middle of a block, Lish said, "Here we are." She started up some round stepping stones that led across a square of grass to a neat blue door. We rang the bell.

No one came to the door, but someone shouted, "Come in! The door's open!"

We stepped inside into a little square hallway. Right in front of us was a stairway.

There was another shout. "Hello! Who is it?"

"Me, Rusty. Lish. And a girl called Consuelo. She's got some papers for you."

"Come on up."

At the top of the stairs I saw the boy who had flown paper airplanes from his balcony the day I arrived. He had a round face and kind of round brown eyes. He seemed kind of round all over, but I really couldn't tell. He was in a wheelchair. His right leg was in a white cast and stuck straight out in front of him. He wheeled himself back and around and through a door in the rear of the house.

"Let's go in my room," he said.

"What happened to your crutches?" Lish asked.

Rusty wrinkled up his face. "I know I should be using them, but I hate them."

Once in the room, I handed him the papers. "I'm Consuelo Harburton," I said. "Mrs. Kessler sent these. They're some student-body stuff for you to fill out."

"Thanks," he said. Then he frowned. "I've never seen you before. How come *you* brought them?"

"Because I'm in your home room. And because I'm living in Shadywood for a while." I looked from the window to the boy in the wheelchair. "Anyway, you *have* seen me before. I guess you're not a monster, but

❧❧❧

you sure looked like one with your face pressed against the glass yesterday. You're the guy who yelled at me."

"Was that you in the tree? Well, just be glad I yelled. Those branches break if you look at them."

I shrugged. I certainly didn't agree with him, but this was no time to argue.

"What were you trying to do, anyway?" Rusty said.

"Get a look at the movie lot. I've never seen one before."

He wheeled over to the window with Lish behind him. "Look all you want," he said. "From here you can see the whole back lot. See there? I figure that's a street in New York a long time ago. And over there's a castle with a drawbridge. They're all fake, of course. Nothing behind them but the back fence. Except for the fort. Looks like they had to build three sides of that."

"Some of New York is falling down," I said.

"And the drawbridge is lopsided," Lish said. "But it doesn't matter. I hear they're going to tear it down pretty soon."

"I know," Rusty moaned. "That's my problem. I've gotta get my stuff out of there."

"What stuff?" Lish asked.

"Two of my cameras. My dad'll kill me if he finds out I've lost them."

"Get Domino to get them," Lish said.

"Domino would, but he can't get in. The place we used to get through's all nailed up."

"Wouldn't somebody let you in?" I said.

"There's nobody to ask."

"Can't your friend climb a tree? He could squirm out on that branch and then drop down to the ground on the other side."

"No way. I tried it. I didn't even make it to your branch." He pointed to his cast. "How do you think I wound up like this?"

"Well, that takes care of that," Lish said.

Not for me, I thought, but I didn't say that. What I said was, "I've got to be going. My grandmother might be home already."

Downstairs a door slammed. A man's voice called, "Russ, I'm back. You okay?"

"Fine, Dad. Some friends are here. But they're just leaving."

❧❦❧

We met Mr. Neeland in the front hall. He had a "happy-day" face. You know, round, with round glasses and a big curved smile.

"Hello, Lish," he said. And then to me, "You must be the Harburton girl. I've just been talking to your grandmother."

He opened the door for us and tapped my shoulder. "See you tonight," he said.

"Oh?"

"There's a special council meeting tonight. At eight o'clock. At your house."

"About Juan Pablo?" I asked.

"Among other things," he said, grinning. "You learn things fast, young lady."

"I guess." I figured that was Mr. Neeland's way of calling me nosy. Who cares? Maybe I am.

Tag is nosy, too. I learned that later that day. Supper that night was fried chicken that Grace brought home in plastic cartons. It was okay. Maybe even good. But I missed the salsa and warm tortillas. Grace was in a hurry because of the council meeting, so I cleaned up the dishes. Then Tag and I went and sat at the top of the stairway. That's when I learned he was nosy.

Each time the doorbell rang, Tag raced
down the stairs and beat Grace to the door.
By the time three men, including Mr. Neeland, and one lady had shown up, Tag
looked worn out from running up and down
the stairs so much.

Then the door bell rang again. This time
Tag went down the steps more slowly. When
I saw who it was, I shrank back against the
wall, but not soon enough. Mr. Ugly Crane
was at the open door. He looked up the
stairs, and when he saw me I swear he
choked. Then he turned to my grandmother
and said, "What's that girl doing here?"

"Do you mean Consuelo?" Grace asked,
aiming a smile at me. "She lives here. She's
my granddaughter."

I didn't hear what Mr. Crane said because
he kind of swallowed his words, but I saw
his face. It was red as a stop light.

Grace is president, or chairman, or something, of the Shadywood Knolls Council.
When she started the meeting, Tag came
and sat beside me again. He listened with
me for a while. I think he would have stayed
awake if I hadn't scratched behind his ears.

I stopped scratching and leaned forward when I heard the name, Juan Pablo.

It was Mr. Crane talking. Anyone would recognize that voice. "About Juan Pablo," he said, "I want to say right up front that you're making a mountain out of a molehill. He's probably just gone home to Mexico."

"Home?" Grace said. "His home is here. He was born here. But wherever he is, we have to find him. He has the master keys to every one of our houses."

"No wonder things have been disappearing." That was Mr. Crane again.

"You can't have it both ways, Chester," Mr. Neeland said. "Either he's gone to Mexico or he's here, stealing our things. Now which is it?"

"What's been stolen?" Grace asked.

"All kinds of things," the other lady answered. "TV's, computers, silver. And Mrs. Leonard on Red Bridge Road lost a fur coat. Although her husband claims it's in storage."

"Well," Grace said, "that certainly has nothing to do with Juan Pablo. I'm really worried about him. It isn't like him to stay away like this."

"Has anyone called his wife?" Mr. Crane asked.

"Chester, you've forgotten," Mr. Neeland said. "His wife died last year. And his son and daughter are on the east coast. There's no one to miss him but us."

"Shouldn't we report him missing?" That was the lady again.

"We'll have to," Grace said. "But shall we wait another day or so? He may return."

They took a vote. They must have raised hands because I didn't hear any yesses or noes. "All right," Grace said. "We'll wait. Now, what about the deficit? Is it serious enough to change our Halloween plans?"

I got up and went to bed then. "Deficit" has something to do with money and numbers. Not enough of either, I think, and it's boring stuff. As to Halloween, I might have listened to what the grown-ups were planning. But what for? I intended to be back home by then.

Chapter Six

After school the next day when I heard, "Consuelo! Wait for me! I'll walk with you," I knew it would be Lish. Things were going right for me all day. The English teacher actually smiled at me. Two girls from Social Studies asked me to have lunch with them. And would anyone believe it? The girl with the mile-long lashes who had frowned at me the day before gave me a smile as she went by our table. This had to be the day I explored the back lot.

Lish and I had walked only a little way when I said, "As soon as we get home, I'm going to go take a look at the old movie lot."

"You are? How?"

"I'm going to climb the tree by Rusty's back wall and drop over."

"You wouldn't!"

"Why not? I've climbed trees taller than that back home. And we're not as heavy as Rusty."

"What do you mean, 'we?'"

"Don't you want to see the back lot before they tear it all down?"

"Sure, but..." Lish's face was all pink again and she shoved her hair over her shoulder. I guess she does that when she's nervous. "I'm not sure my folks would like that. Would your grandmother let you?"

I shrugged. "She hasn't said I can't."

Lish grinned. "Nobody's told me to keep out of there either. But that's an awfully big tree. I'm not sure I can climb it."

"Nothing to it," I said. "I'll show you how." I know I sounded pretty sure of myself, but I was. My cousin Rebecca, who is a year older than I am, taught me how to climb. Not that I wasn't afraid, but Rebecca can talk you into anything. I sure do miss her.

❧❦❧

Right now as I looked at Lish I wasn't at all sure she would go with me, but when we were at the walk-in gate she said, "All right, I'll do it. But hurry up before I change my mind."

At the tree I went first and gave Lish a hand up. Rusty sure must have been clumsy. We didn't have any trouble, even when we climbed out on the branch. It bent just enough for an easy jump to the ground. I did lose my balance though and ended up on my hands and knees.

As I stood up, I felt the locket around my neck slide down to my waist. I dug under my shirt and pulled it out. Sure enough, the chain had broken. But I wasn't too worried. That had happened before and Rebecca and I had fixed it with a pair of Tío Fernando's pliers. I stuffed the locket into my pocket and said, "Let's go see the fort."

I wanted to go right to the fort and find a way into the tower, but Lish said, "You got me here, so I get to choose. I want to see the castle first."

"Okay, Let's go."

The castle was up against the back fence, maybe two blocks away. The fort was halfway there, to our left. New York was on the other side and closer. We went right by it.

"Look, Lish, look! Posts for tying up your horses."

They were on the street in front of a newspaper office, a ladies' hat store, and a tobacco shop. There were big hats piled with flowers painted on the hat store's phony window and a big pipe was on a sign that hung by the tobacco shop's door.

Lish nudged me. "Did they really wear hats like that?"

"Probably," I said. "But how would I know? I wasn't there." Lish giggled and so did I, even though what I'd said wasn't all that funny.

Next to the tobacco shop was a painted outside stairway. Even this close up you got the feeling that you could climb those steps. It was weird.

The wooden sidewalk in front of the shops creaked and shook as we walked on it.

"This is creepy," Lish said. "Maybe we shouldn't be here."

"Why?"

"I don't know. I feel as if we're being watched."

"That's silly," I said. But I looked over my shoulder anyway. And my heart jumped a foot. Somebody's head was poked out of the tobacco shop's door. When I looked again, it was gone. Maybe I imagined it. "That's silly," I said again to Lish, and we walked toward the castle.

The drawbridge was real. Made of heavy boards and real chains that were connected to posts behind the fake stone front. The moat wasn't much. Sort of a dried-out little gully. But the huge boulders at the edge were great. They were made of some kind of cardboard, shaped and painted. We learned that when we tried climbing on them. Boy, did they look real.

Lish wanted to look behind, inside and under everything. I think she was looking for Rusty's stuff.

"Come on," I said. "If you're going to find anything, it'll be in the fort."

On the way there we walked on the other side of the lot, away from New York. I don't know why we did that, we just did. From that distance everything over there really looked real. I kept expecting the tobacco shop's door to open. But it didn't.

The fort was great. Real logs for the walls. The big double gates were hanging crookedly, as if they had broken hinges. But they were partially open and we walked in. Rusty was right. They had built three sides of the fort. The fourth side was nothing but the regular movie lot fence. There were some real rooms built on both sides of the gate. And there were stairs that led up to a walkway above them and to the tower. That's where I wanted to go. But Lish had other ideas.

"Maybe Rusty's camera is in one of these rooms. Let's look."

"You look. I'm going to the tower."

"I want to see the tower, too," Lish said. "But we're down here now. Let's do this first."

So that's what we did. We opened the door to the room under the tower. No windows, of course, so it was dark. But with the door wide open, we could see that it was filled with stuff. Boxes and ladders and cans of all sizes. It was going to take some careful dodging not to bump into anything.

I stopped and sniffed. "Do you smell oranges?" I whispered.

"Do you?" Lish whispered back.

"I guess not. But why are we whispering?"

"I don't know," Lish said in a normal voice.

I moved a couple of cans around. "Paint," I said. "This is just a storeroom. Let's go to the tower."

I turned toward the open door, but stopped again. "Hey," I whispered, "what's on that box by the door?"

I didn't have to ask. Now that my eyes were more used to the dark, I could see pretty well. It was a basket half-filled with large oranges. Orange peels were scattered on the floor beside the box. "I knew I smelled oranges," I said. "Look."

Lish went to the basket and took an orange. "Oh, good," she said. "I'm starving."

"Put it back, Lish. They're not ours."

"Nobody'll miss it. I'll spread the others out." She threw an orange to me and I just barely caught it.

"Lish!" I was whispering again. "You know what that means. Somebody else has been here. Maybe they're still here. Let's get out."

I walked to the basket, tossed the orange into it and pulled in my breath. In the bottom, almost hidden by the rest of the oranges, was an envelope with "Mrs. Harburton" written on it.

Lish, the orange she had taken still in her hand, was looking behind the box, so I quickly folded the envelope and pushed it into my pants pocket. Or tried to. I dragged it out again.

"Did you hear that?" Lish whispered.

"What?"

"Kind of a clinking sound."

"A what?" I wanted to keep her talking while I folded the envelope tighter and shoved it back into my pocket. Maybe I should have felt sneaky taking it, but, after all, it was addressed to my grandmother.

"Oh, forget it," Lish said.

✺✺✺

"We'd better go," I said, whirling around. "Come on."

Just as I said that, something furry touched my arm, and my heart jumped again. It wasn't anything scary, though. Just a huge paint brush on a crate behind me. Even so, my heart didn't get a chance to go back where it belonged. Because from straight above us someone screamed, "Ay-eee-eee-ay!"

Lish didn't wait for me. She made a choking noise and ran out the door and through the gate. I caught up with her. In fact, I beat her to the spot where we'd come over the fence. But when I got there, I stopped dead in my tracks. On this side of the fence there was no tree to climb.

Chapter Seven

"We can't go this way!" Lish screeched.

"I know! Come on!"

I ran away from the tower and from the fort, and Lish followed me. We stayed close to the fence. The Shadywood buildings were *so* close, but what good did that do us? The fence was so high. I was sure I'd been running for miles when I came to a corner in the fence. I stopped, trying to catch my breath. I looked back at the fort. "No one's... chasing... us," I panted. "I'm not... gonna... run anymore."

Lish didn't say anything. She nodded.

My stomach felt funny. Squiggly. If this had happened back home, Rebecca would have been with me telling me what to do. Rebecca had always been there, way before either one of us could walk. But here I was on my own, and I wasn't sure I liked it. I didn't like walking so near the back side of New York either. I told myself I wasn't scared, just careful, but my stomach stayed squiggly anyway. Who knows how much worse my stomach might have gotten, but right then I had an idea.

The fence was eight-feet high and made of six-inch wide boards. After we turned the corner, I pushed at every board, hoping I could pry one loose. Pretty soon Lish got the idea. She pushed at the bottom while I pushed at the top. But that was hard on our hands. By the time we were near the back fence, we were pounding the boards with a couple of big rocks. The rocks made loud thumping sounds, loud enough so that Tía Alma would have said we were "awakening the dead." So I kept looking around. Nobody was following us, but I had the weird feeling that we were being watched. I shuddered. We had to get out of there before it got dark.

☙❧

"What's the use?" Lish said. "This isn't working. We should find something to stand on so we can get *over* the fence."

I looked unhappily at the clutter of old sticks, broken wooden frames, empty crates and other junk piled against the back of New York. "Sure. Like what?"

Lish shrugged.

I found a bigger rock and went at the next board in the fence with all my might. "Lish," I cried, "look! This board's moving!"

"Wait for me," Lish said, and picked up her rock again.

We both beat on the fence. In a few minutes the board we were pounding squeaked as it pulled away from the nails on the cross piece. The fence board next to it gave a little, too. We pounded and hammered and soon we had loosened them both enough so we could push them out, lift them and wiggle our way through. Boy, did it feel good to be on the other side of that fence.

I looked around. We were on an old street that didn't go anywhere. It ended against a couple of little hills covered with dry, brown weeds.

❧

"This way!" Lish said, and we started running away from the hills.

I thought of something. "Wait, Lish, stop! We'd better put some kind of a mark on the boards we loosened."

"What for?"

I wasn't sure. But now that we'd found a way in, I didn't want to lose it. "For Rusty," I said. "So his friend, Domino, can look for his cameras."

"So long as it's not for me. Go on. I'll wait for you."

I ran back and scratched an "X" on each board with a sharp rock. Then we started walking. It took a while to reach the front entrance of Shadywood Knolls. We said hello to the man in the gatehouse. Then we went to Blue Stone Road and took a shortcut between two buildings to where we'd left our bookbags. We got them and turned to leave, but stopped when we heard a yell.

"Hey, you guys! I saw you over there!" It was Rusty, his face pressed against the window screen. "How'd you get out? Come on up and tell me."

When we were up in his room, Rusty said, "Last I saw you, you were turning the corner by New York. Did you find my cameras?"

"No," Lish said. "Sorry."

I frowned. "How did you know it was us? Anyway, isn't the tree in the way?"

Rusty, who was hobbling around on crutches this time, pointed to a pair of binoculars on his desk. "I just dug these out this afternoon. I can see a lot with them, even through the branches."

"You mean you've been watching us?" Lish asked. "Did you see anybody else?"

"No," Rusty said. "Should I?"

"The scream!" I practically shouted. "Someone screamed in the fort!"

That did it. Rusty had to hear everything. We finished by telling him how we'd marked the fence boards. "Wow," he said when we were through. "I wonder what's going on over there."

"That's what I'd like to know," I said. And scared as I still was, I meant it.

Lish went to the window. "I don't see anything moving over there right now. Yes, I do. But it's just a cat. A pretty one, though. All sorts of colors. You know, like a crazy quilt. Do you suppose that's what we heard? A cat yowling?"

"Sure," I said with a shrug. "A crazy-quilt cat that peels oranges and eats them."

Rusty laughed and Lish tossed her hair over her shoulder. Then she turned and grinned at me.

I said, "I'm sorry about your cameras, Rusty, but I don't know about going back there again."

Rusty said, "Domino will go. Especially now that you've got a way in and out. I'm going to school tomorrow. I'll talk to him."

I wasn't sure that Domino, whoever he was, would be in such a hurry to go there when Rusty told him what we'd heard. But, if he did, I hoped he had better luck than we did.

"All right then," Rusty said, "let's talk more at lunch tomorrow. The only good thing about these crutches is that I get in the cafeteria early. I'll save places for you."

We left then. When I turned on to Woodside Lane, I saw right away that Grace was home. The garage door was wide open. Would she be mad at me for coming home so late? I dragged my feet as I walked toward the house. Back home in Dos Palos the bus always got us home from school on time. One day last year Rebecca and I missed it, and not only did we get a red hot scolding, we weren't allowed to watch television that night.

I let myself in the front door and dropped my bookbag to the floor. I was about to go up the stairs when I heard a man's voice. And the voice I heard made me forget about being late and about the movie lot and the talk we'd had with Rusty.

The man was saying, "Things are much better now. *Gracias a Dios.*"

Grace said, "Yes, thank God" in English, and I rushed in the room.

"Tío Fernando," I cried joyfully, "you've come to get me!"

Chapter Eight

Two steps inside the doorway I stopped. I felt as if someone had hit me in the stomach. The man sitting stiffly on a straight-backed chair facing my grandmother was a stranger.

"But... but... but you sounded like Tío Fernando," I stammered, hot tears starting in the back of my eyes.

The man in the chair stood up and Grace came and put her arm around my shoulders. "This is Juan Pablo, honey," she said. And then, "Juan Pablo, this is my granddaughter, Consuelo. She's come to live with me."

The man called Juan Pablo nodded and smiled down at me. He had sad-looking brown eyes and a smile that seemed sad, too. But when he spoke all of that changed. "What a pleasure to meet you, *señorita* Consuelo," he said. His smile became a broad grin. "So you two have found each other? I don't know which of you is the luckiest."

You mean luckier, I thought. I was being as picky as my English teacher, and I knew why. I was feeling pretty stupid about busting in the way I had, and I had to be mad at somebody. I didn't say anything, though. I just stood there and blinked.

Juan Pablo picked up a hat from a table by his chair. "Thank you, señora Harburton," he said. "Maybe someday we'll find out about the basket of oranges and the note I left in them."

Oranges and a note. I didn't need a computer to work that one out. I swallowed hard as I started to dig in my pocket for the letter I'd put there. I swallowed again and drew my hand back. If I couldn't get rid of the lump in my throat, how could I explain where I'd found it?

Grace was talking. "Maybe I'll learn to check my answering machine before I leave on a trip. I have no idea why I had turned it off. But all's well that ends well. I'm glad you're back, Juan Pablo."

I just stood there as the door closed behind him. Then I said, "Where was he?" I asked that question not so much because I wanted to know the answer but because I didn't want Grace to talk about my calling him Tío Fernando. And she didn't.

"Juan Pablo," she said, "flew to New York. His daughter had emergency surgery. A bad appendix. But she's out of danger now. Well, come help me start dinner. I thought we'd have spaghetti and a salad. Is that all right?"

"Sure. Let me put my bookbag away." I went up to my room slowly. I was still struggling with my disappointment. If only that had been Tío Fernando. But I had to forget that now. I had to go down and give Grace the letter.

I dug in my back pocket and pulled out the envelope. Then I reached for my locket and everything changed. My pocket was empty, entirely empty. My locket was gone! I sat on the edge of the bed. The desk and chair and chest of drawers muttered, "Gone, gone, gone," and pretty soon the sun crashed through the roof. Or that's how it seemed. I tried hard to remember. Where had I lost it? How? And then it came to me. "Kind of a clinking sound," Lish had said when I was wrestling with the envelope in the fort. That had to be when I'd dropped my locket. Tomorrow, no matter what, I had to go into the movie lot and get it.

Finally, I remembered that Grace was waiting. I stood up and looked in the envelope. It was just what I thought: a note from Juan Pablo saying that he had to leave for a couple of days and that he was sure she'd understand. I stared at the note in my hand. If I gave it to her, then she'd know I'd been over in the movie lot.

What if she said I couldn't go back there again? And now I had to. That locket was important. A year ago when I had fixed it up with my parents' pictures and put it around my neck, I felt so much better that right then and there I swore always to wear it. *I couldn't lose it*. Anyway, Grace already knew what it said. I put the envelope under my socks in the middle drawer and told myself I'd give it to her later.

I went downstairs then. The spaghetti was good, but I couldn't eat much. The lump in my throat had returned.

The next day when I got to the cafeteria, Rusty was there, waving his arms like mad so I could see him. Lish wasn't there yet, but someone else was. The boy who had been at the far corner table yesterday was sitting by the girl with the mile-long lashes.

Rusty said, "Hi, Counsel."

"Consuelo," I said quickly, giving the boy next to him a look. Did he remember me?

"Yeah, right," Rusty said. "Counsel, this is my friend, Domino."

Domino said, "You might as well get used to 'Counsel.' He'll call you that from now on. My name's really Domingo.

"Mine's really Consuelo," I said.

"That's my mother's name, too," Domingo said, and his face got red. "Now I know why you took your lunch tray and left yesterday. You knew what we said in Spanish."

Lish arrived just then. She plopped her tray on the table and said, "Did you tell

Domingo all about it? Have you made any plans?"

"Plans?" Domingo asked. "For what?"

"To get my cameras from the back lot," Rusty said, "and find out what's going on over there. Remember, I didn't just forget my cameras. I put them down by the tobacco shop in New York, and when I turned around they were gone."

So Domingo had to hear our story. Lish and Rusty told most of it. I just nodded and finally said, "We were lucky to find a way out."

"There's something mysterious going on in that movie lot," Rusty said. "Last night about ten-thirty I saw a light in the fort. It wasn't much of a light, just a sliver along a window. And then it was gone."

"Where?" I asked quickly. "In the tower?"

Rusty shook his head. "No, in one of the ground-floor rooms just past the gate."

Where my locket is, I thought, holding back a groan. What I said was, "Well, it looks like there's something over there that swipes cameras, peels oranges and turns on lights."

"Yeah," Rusty said. "What else do we know?"

"Who cares?" Lish said.

"Domingo probably does," I said. "And so do I. I'd like to find out what's happening there."

Rusty said, "Me, too. So let's put what we know together."

We all talked at once. Even Lish. The trouble was that we kept repeating the same things. What we finally added was the scream in the fort and what I had overheard in the council meeting about what had been stolen. And that wasn't much.

Domingo said, "What does the stolen stuff have to do with the movie lot? Probably nothing."

"Maybe not," Lish said. "So who is over there? I know we heard someone."

"Someone who is hurting," Domingo said. "What we should do is help them."

"I don't think so," I said.

Domingo gave me a surprised look, but I went on anyway. "If they needed help, they'd ask for it. They wouldn't just peek around

corners at us. I'm pretty sure there was someone in the tobacco shop."

"What if they're scared to ask for help?"
Domingo said, his face getting red. "What if
they're scared they'd be deported?"

Lish spoke up. "I don't think it's anything
like that. Maybe it's homeless people. And they
wouldn't want anyone to know they're there
'cause they'd get kicked out."

"Well, we're never going to find out what's
really going on by just talking about it," Rusty
said. "You guys have to go over there and find
out."

"That's easy for you to say," Lish said. "I'm
not sure I want to go over there. Anyway, even
if I wanted to, I can't today. I have my piano
lesson."

"I can't either," Domingo said. "I've got to
baby-sit my kid brothers."

"Well, tomorrow then," Rusty said. It
looked to me as if he'd appointed himself our
leader. "Meanwhile, I'll keep checking the
place with my binoculars."

I just sat and said nothing. Tomorrow was
too late for me. I couldn't wait that long to find
my locket. I'd just have to go over there alone.

Chapter Nine

When I got home after school that day, Grace was waiting for me.

"How would you like to go down to the mall?" she said. "To buy you some new tees and a sweater, maybe?"

I frowned. I *know* I did. I wanted new clothes, all right, but not today. Today there was something I wanted more. I said, "That's nice of you, Grace, but I don't need anything yet, do I? You sent me a box full of things this summer. Could we go another day?"

Grace raised one eyebrow—how did she do that?—and just looked at me for a minute. Then she said, "All right. I have some phone calls to catch up with. I can use the time."

She smiled at me as she said that, but there was something in her voice that didn't go with the smile. Something kind of mixed up and sad. I started up the stairs.

Before I reached the top, Grace called, "There's a letter for you. I left it on your dresser."

A letter? For me? It had to be from Dos Palos. I raced the rest of the way and tore open the envelope. It was from Rebecca.

"I know it's only Monday," she wrote, "and you just left Saturday, but I had to write to tell you that I've decided that you have to come back home again. It's not right here without you. Monica is hard to live with and the twins ask what you're doing every half-hour.

"I have a plan I'm working on that I call 'Return Consuelo.' Part of it is to convince my parents to write your grandmother and explain how much you need us. But that's only part of it. I'll write you more about it in a day or two.

"There's a new boy in school. But I won't tell you about him because you'll get to meet him yourself. 'Return Consuelo' is going to work."

Rebecca added a P.S. "Wouldn't it be nice if we both had computers with e-mail?"

I put the letter down. Rebecca's letter made me homesick. But right now I had to think of just one thing. To get into the old movie lot and find my locket.

Downstairs I found my grandmother and said, "Could I take Tag for a walk?"

She looked up from her desk. "I'm sorry, honey, Queen Isabella's got him. She walks him every afternoon. I pay her a little something, and I hate to take the job away from her. Do you mind?"

"Uh-uh," I said. "I'll just go catch up with them."

Grace seemed pleased. I felt a little guilty as I closed the door behind me. Because, of course, I had no intention of looking for Queenie. I hurried up Woodside Lane toward the gatehouse. I had gone only a block or so when I saw Juan Pablo. He appeared from the side of a house, a tool box in his hand. I buried my chin in my chest and walked fast, hoping he wouldn't recognize me. But he did.

"Buenas tardes, señorita Consuelo," he called.

I turned. *"Buenas tardes, señor."* He grinned and I added in Spanish, "It's nice that you can talk Spanish."

"And you, too," he said.

"My grandmother doesn't. She only knows English."

Juan Pablo shook his head slowly. "No, no, not only English. Señora Harburton speaks the best language of all."

"She *does?* What's that?"

"Call it 'people talk,'" he said. "But I'm sure it has a better name than that."

"Oh," I said with a shrug, because I really didn't know what he meant, "I guess I'd better go."

Juan Pablo said, *"Adiós,"* and I walked fast until he was out of sight.

Then I raced past the gatehouse and around the corner toward the movie lot's side fence and the low hills. Once I'd turned the corner, it didn't take long to get there. A strong breeze had sprung up and it gave me a boost.

I had no trouble finding the fence boards that I'd marked. But getting in was another matter. This time I had to pry the boards away from the nails and pull them toward me, and that was harder than pushing against them with your body. Finally, I was able to lift the boards up enough to let me squirm through. I straightened up and looked around. Well, here I was in the back lot again, but this time I was all alone.

I guess I could have taken a short cut to the fort, but that meant going through one of the phony shop doors or walking between the New York buildings. Somehow that didn't appeal to me. Especially since the sea breeze was causing a lot of creaking and groaning in New York, and that was kind of creepy. So I walked along the fence. I looked for my locket with every step, even though I was sure I'd dropped it in the fort.

When I got to the fort I stopped for a minute and looked at the gates. They were hanging at a crooked angle just like before, only now they were not as far open. Maybe the wind had closed them. Or maybe the "orange eaters." Now that I was here I was scared. Whoever was in there didn't want anyone around. Still, Domingo had said that it was someone who was hurting. Maybe whoever it was *did* want help.

I knew all this thinking was just stalling for time, so I made myself take a few steps toward the gate, stopped, then took a few more. It's a good thing I went slowly because just as I reached the gate I heard men's voices. I pressed myself tight against the log wall, trying to be absolutely still. But I had to breathe. And every breath I took sounded like a windstorm. They didn't hear me, though, because they kept on talking. I couldn't hear words. One voice was deep and gruff. In a few seconds their words were clear. They must have been coming down the steps from the tower.

"Hey, stupid," the gruff one said, "where d'ya think you're going?"

"Jeez, Nick," the other man whined, "I'm not cut out to be a shut-in. I figured I'd get a little air."

"You'll get a little air, all right. A nice, neat bullet hole right through the chest unless you cut out the crap. We'll go out when we've moved these things upstairs."

That's when my heart jumped into my throat, changed its mind and plummeted down to my stomach. *They had guns!*

"Okay, okay, Nick," the second man said, "but maybe we'd better wait till dark. Those damn kids keep popping up about this time."

"Not anymore," Gruff Voice answered. "I took care of that. Did you ever see anyone move faster than that little blonde yesterday?" He laughed and it sounded as if he'd slapped his leg. "I think I've got me a career in horror movies."

So the scream hadn't been real. If I hadn't been so scared, I would've been mad. But I was. Too scared to move. Scared they'd hear me if I ran, because now there was a dead silence. I stood there, chewing my lip, wondering what to do, when I heard a great stirring in the air above me. I jumped and drew in my breath as harsh cries, "Carr! Carr! Carr!," tore through the silence.

My heart was getting its exercise today. Now it was beating furiously as it leaped into my mouth. I closed my eyes and willed the awful noise to go away. When it didn't I leaned carefully away from my wall and looked up. At least five black crows were perched on the sides and top of the tower, each cawing louder than the other. Crows. If I hadn't been so terrified, I would have known. After all, we have them in Dos Palos, too. Those ugly black crows had almost scared the life out of me, but even so, I was glad for them. With all the noise they were making, no one was going to hear me. I ran.

I started toward the fence and changed my mind. The quickest way out of here was through New York. And that's where I headed. But when I reached the wooden sidewalk I stopped dead in my tracks.

There were no spaces between the buildings. The dark alleyways were painted on, too. The whole block of shops was a solid wooden facade. Still, I was sure that the tobacco store had a door that opened. Someone's head had peeked out of it yesterday. I remembered that. I raced to it, pulled open a real door with a real doorknob and found myself looking down at a little girl in a bright red tee shirt.

Chapter Ten

She was sitting on a box, her head flung back, her eyes wide with fear. "Oh," she said in a high little voice, "you're not them."

I waited until I had caught my breath to respond. "Who's them?" I said.

"The two men in the fort. I thought they were chasing me."

"I was afraid they were chasing me, too," I said, and looked out a crack by the door, "but they're not." I peered through the crack again. "No one's there," I said and looked around.

We were in a closed-in little space, the walls made of boards and large sections of cardboard leaning on empty wooden crates.

❧❧

Three or four upturned boxes were in a semi-circle. The girl was seated on one of them. She looked to be about ten. She was small-boned, with black hair that was shiny and short and straight as a pencil. Her eyes, too, were black, and slanted. I thought she was very pretty. Now I noticed something else. She was hunched over with both hands holding her ankle.

"Is something wrong?" I asked.

She nodded. "I twisted my ankle on that ancient wooden sidewalk, and it's remarkably painful."

She certainly didn't sound like a ten-year-old. "Do you think it's broken?" I asked.

"No. I've twisted it before. But I can't stand on it. I'm sure of that. And I want to get out of here."

"So do I, but I don't want them to see me."

The girl sighed. "It's a dilemma, isn't it?"

I nodded. "My name's Consuelo," I said, because I couldn't think of anything better to say. "What's yours?"

"It *was* O-lan," she said, "but my new name is Ellen, Ellen Marie."

꧁꧂

"O-lan," I said slowly. "Is that Chinese?"

She crinkled her black eyes at me in a big smile. "It's Chinese, yes. When I was a baby, I was Chinese, but now I'm Chinese and American." She rubbed her ankle and said, "Dear jewel of heaven, why did I have to be so clumsy?"

I turned and glanced through the crack. There was no one in the lot between the fort and where we were. "Do you think you could walk if you leaned on me?"

"I'm sure I could, thank you. But I'll be able to walk alone as soon as I rest a while."

"Okay," I said, and sat on a box near her. I watched her rub her ankle for a minute and then I said, "What're you doing here?"

"I came to retrieve something. Something I left behind."

My mouth dropped open. "Retrieve." Who ever used words like that? "Here?" I asked.

"Not *precisely* here," she said. "In the fort. I left my bookbag there yesterday."

"Yesterday? After school?"

She nodded. "I saw you and Alicia there. I was in that room downstairs, too. When you came in, I hid behind some packing cases."

"You mean Lish and I scared you?"

"Not when I saw who you were. Actually, I was planning to scare *you* when that devastating scream came and you ran out of there. So did I. Only I went the other way. Toward the castle. And in my haste and confusion I left my bookbag." She closed her eyes again and her mouth trembled a little. "All those books," she said in a shaky little voice. "They are entirely too expensive. And my parents are not at all wealthy."

All the time she was talking I was hearing her, but I was thinking, too. "All right," I said, "then we have to go back there. I left something, too. A locket. It's kind of important."

"But is it wise?" the girl called Ellen said. "Those men have taken possession of the fort."

I gave her a long look. No one, *no one,* talked like that. Except in books. "I know," I said. "But I heard them talking. They said they were going somewhere in a little while. I'll bet anything they're gone by now. How's your ankle?"

She stood up and took a couple of steps. "Much, much better. I think I can walk. I'll just have to be especially careful."

"So should we go?"

"I suppose so. We're being very brave, aren't we?"

I shrugged. "I guess so."

So we went back to the fort. It took us a long time because we didn't go across the empty space between it and New York. No. We hugged the fence by Shadywood like two scared rabbits, stopping every little while to study the old log buildings for a sign of the two men and to rest Ellen's ankle. When we were right across from the fort, we went as quickly as we could to the wall by the gate.

We listened. We looked. And, finally, after much whispering and making signs and faces, we edged around the gate and went inside. We listened again. Not a sound. We tiptoed slowly to the storeroom door. All of a sudden I wanted to turn around and run. I closed my eyes tight and squeezed some courage into my jumpy heart.

I leaned close to Ellen's ear and whispered, "I don't hear anything."

"Neither do I," she whispered back.

"All right then," I said, "let's go in."

Except for the same old boxes and stuff, the room was empty. Ellen made a beeline between the boxes to the back of the room. I turned to the crate beside the door where the oranges had been. And still were. Only there were fewer of them. And more peelings on the floor. I got down on my hands and knees, moved the peelings around with my hand, and, glinting beneath them, I found my locket.

I almost wished I hadn't. Because there wasn't much left of it. Someone had stepped on it hard. Before this, my locket had opened like a little book. Now, one-half of it was gone and the other half was flattened out of shape, with only my father's smudged face still grinning up at me.

I sat and stared at the locket for a little bit. But staring didn't help. Nothing changed. It was still all smashed up. I picked it up and put it in my pocket. Then I pushed myself off the floor and went looking for Ellen.

"Hey," I whispered, "where are you?"

"Here." Her voice came softly from a far corner. "They threw my bag behind these enormous containers and, oh, dear, I don't know if it's possible to reach it."

She had somehow climbed on top of a huge box and was leaning over into the dark corner beyond it.

I said, "Let me see. Maybe I can help."

"Would you, please? I'll just get down off..." She didn't finish.

We stared at one another for a second and then we both looked up at the ceiling. Footsteps. Heavy footsteps. Someone was up in the tower, someone who might be coming down any minute. "Get down," I whispered. "Let's get out of here."

She slid off the box and we walked quickly and quietly out of the storeroom, past the steps to the tower and through the gate. We stayed close to the fence for a while and then made a dash—as much of a dash as Ellen's ankle would allow—to New York and the tobacco shop door. We opened and closed the door fast and, once inside, both of us took long, deep breaths.

❧❧

Ellen started to say something, but stopped. She frowned, shook her head and finally said, "They are exceedingly bad men, aren't they?"

"They sure are."

"Are they too dangerous for us to confront them?"

I stared at her. Confront? What was she thinking of? "Of course they are," I said.

"Well, then, my books are lost. And I am in desperate trouble."

"I'm sorry. About the books, I mean."

"My desperate trouble is not about books. It's about disobedience. My parents have forbidden me to enter this place, and with the schoolbooks gone, I will have to tell them I've been here. They will say, 'O-lan'—they always call me 'O-lan when I have disappointed them—'O-lan, how shall we punish you?' And they will expect me to give up television and also Sherlock Holmes."

"Sherlock Holmes? Sherlock Holmes, the detective?"

"Yes. I'm reading every one of his books," Ellen said with a little nod. "They are entirely wonderful."

❦❦

I gave her a questioning look. She was serious. "Oh, Ellen," I said, "I'm very sorry."

"I believe you," she said. And then, "Did you find what you were looking for?"

"Kind of. It was a locket, but it's ruined."

"A locket," she said. "And it was a treasure, wasn't it?" I nodded because I had trouble talking and Ellen said, "That's truly a tragedy."

I nodded again. "I have to go now," I blurted out.

She said, "We can go out this way," and pushed aside some of the boards that made up the wall of the enclosure.

We squeezed between the wooden crates and walked along the side fence until we came to where the loose fence boards were.

"This is the way I got in," I said. "How about you?"

"Through the fence behind the castle. It's closer to where I live. Thank you for your help. I'll look for you tomorrow."

"You will? Where?"

"At school."

"Do you go to Franklin Middle?"

"Of course. And so do you." She waved a quick good-bye and kept going toward the back of the lot.

Ellen disappeared behind the castle as I pushed through the fence. All the way home I thought sadly of the tiny-boned girl in the red tee shirt and of her "desperate trouble." Maybe she was what Rebecca would call a nerd, or a dweeb, or a nutcake, but Rebecca wasn't here to tell me what to think, and I liked her.

Chapter Eleven

As I turned on to Woodside Lane, the gateman called to me, "You'd better hurry, kiddo. Your grandmother's looking for you."

"I will," I called back, and swallowed hard. I'd forgotten all about the time.

Juan Pablo was at the red bridge. He waved and said, "Ah, there you are. Señora Harburton will be glad to see you."

"Oh," I said, and felt my face turn red.

Grace was waiting for me at the front door. "Oh, honey," she said, "I'm so glad to see you. Queenie and Tag returned more than an hour ago, and when they said they hadn't seen you..."

❦❦❦

"I'm sorry," I mumbled. "I'm sorry." And I honestly was. I could see that Grace was really worried about me. I don't know why, but that surprised me.

"Come on in the kitchen," she said. "I have to get the rocks out of the oven before they burn."

Rocks? What I smelled was cinnamony and buttery and made my mouth water. "Why are you cooking rocks?" I asked as I followed her into the kitchen.

Grace laughed. "That's what your father called them. They're really oatmeal cookies, the kind that are best dunked in cold milk. I thought you'd be back in time to help me with them, but... well..."

"I'm sorry," I said again. "Maybe I can help clean up."

"Yes," Grace said. "After we've had a little talk." She pulled out a sheet of cookies from the oven. "Sit down while I put these on paper towels." When she was done, she came and sat on the other side of the little table and faced me. "Now for our talk." She put her elbow on the table, leaned her head on her hand, and said, "Look, Consuelo, you and I are going to be together for many years, so we have to decide how best to get along. And I suggest that being honest with one another is the best way. Do you agree?"

"Sure."

"All right," she said, "then I'll begin."

I looked at Grace's serious face and butterflies began scrambling around in my stomach. I was really going to get a scolding.

Grace sighed. "I've lived alone since your father went off to college, and that's a long time. So it's hard for me to get used to having someone else living with me. Most of the time when I remember that you're here to stay, I'm really happy, but then there are other times. The times when I worry about whether or not *you'll* be happy here. Do you understand what I'm saying?"

"I guess so," I said, my eyes on the rows of oatmeal cookies on the tile drainboard. She sounded just like my father had. He always talked to me as if I was a grown-up. Reasoning, he called it. He didn't like rules. But my mother sure did. Sometimes it was easier to take my mother's scoldings than my father's "reasoning" talks. "I guess so," I repeated.

❧❧❧

"I hope so," Grace said. "Today when you were gone so long I thought something bad had happened. And when the gateman said you'd left Shadywood, I was sure of it. I thought that you... I thought that maybe you'd decided..." She stopped.

She didn't need to finish. I knew what she was thinking. She thought I'd decided to run away. To run away to Dos Palos. "I didn't decide to do anything," I said. "I was just looking for something that I lost, and it got late awful fast."

Grace closed her eyes and took a deep breath.

I said, "I'm sorry if I scared you, honest I am."

My grandmother opened her eyes and smiled at me, and I said, "Why did my father call them rocks? They look really good to me." Grace looked puzzled. "The rocks," I said. "You know, the cookies."

"Oh, dear, the cookies. I'd forgotten. And they're really best when they're warm." She got up. "Your father liked to pretend they were too hard to chew. That's why he called them rocks."

"My mother never made cookies," I said. "She just bought them."

"So do I, most of the time. But I thought ... and then... well, it doesn't matter what I thought. Let's have some milk and cookies."

And, just like with my father, my grandmother's "reasoning" talk kind of conked out then, and I didn't remind her to finish it. When I was through with my milk, I helped her clean up the cookie mess. Then I went up to my room.

Tag came with me, but he wasn't much company. He wagged his tail once or twice and then scrambled up onto my bed and fell asleep. That was okay because I wanted to look at my locket. When I did, I wished I hadn't. I put it under my pillow and tried to put it out of my mind while I did some homework.

At bedtime I pulled it out and whispered good night, but it wasn't the same. I was glad I had my father's picture even if it was all scratched up, but my mother should have been there, too. Besides, it wouldn't go around my neck anymore.

Sure, I had that picture of my folks Tía Alma had taken from her refrigerator. I could cut it up to fit into another locket. But how much would a new locket cost?

I lay back and stared at the ceiling for a long time and then I felt a tear sneaking down the side of my nose. And then another one. I let them. I decided that if God saw me cry, it wouldn't matter, not this time. Anyway, it wasn't as if it was Rebecca watching.

At school the next morning I looked for Ellen, but I didn't see her. Was she really old enough for sixth grade? I know she talked old enough for college, but still, she was awfully little.

During second period Lish passed me a note. "Rusty says meet him in the cafeteria. He has an idea."

I wanted to write a note back because I had an idea, too, but I figured lunchtime would be soon enough to tell her.

Rusty's idea wasn't at all new. The first part of it was that we should look for his cameras all around New York because that's where they'd disappeared. "We'll call it,

'Operation Camera,'" he said. "And I'll keep track of you guys all the time."

Domingo said, "Sure, we'll start there. Why not?"

Lish shook her head. "I'll think about it. About going at all, I mean."

I said, "I've gotta think about it, too." I'm not sure what made me say that, because I knew I would go with Domingo.

The second part of Rusty's idea was the new part. It was a way we could signal him if we *really* got in trouble in the back lot. At first I thought his plan was pretty silly, but after a bit it seemed okay. On the cafeteria table in front of him were three tight rolls of crepe-paper streamers.

"Here," he said, handing one to each of us. "Keep these in your pockets. If you get into real trouble, throw one of the them over a gate or something, somewhere so I can see it. I'll be watching with my binoculars."

"Great," Lish said. "What if we're inside when we need help?"

"Throw the streamer out a window. There are three of you. One of you might get

❧❧❧

the chance. Anyway, it's better than nothing."

Domingo said, "Yeah. Just a little bit better than nothing. But we're not gonna need
help. If I thought we were, I wouldn't be
messing around over there. A couple of
homeless people aren't gonna bite us."

I wanted to say that the men I'd heard
might do more than bite. Instead, I bit my
tongue. Anyway, it was time to tell them my
idea. But I didn't do that either.

Before I could say anything, a voice
behind me said, "Hello, Consuelo. You are
exactly where I expected to find you."

I turned around. Ellen, in a different tee
shirt, but one just as red, was smiling down
at me.

"Hello," I said. "I'm glad you're here. I
was just going to..." I stopped because I saw
the look on Rusty's face. It was not friendly.

Lish said, "Hello, Ellen. Did you find
your Social Studies book?"

"Not yet," Ellen said, "but I will. Perhaps
this afternoon."

Domingo and Rusty exchanged looks,
and I felt as flat as a busted balloon. They'd

never let Ellen be part of our team, and that had been my idea.

Ellen looked down at my empty plate. "Did you have the Spanish rice? It was not exactly appetizing, was it? But I was ravenous, so I ate it all anyway."

I nodded. What else could I do?

She tapped me on the shoulder and said, "I finished reading my current Sherlock Holmes and I've started another. I thought you'd want to know." I nodded again and she said, "Here's the bookmark I promised you."

She handed me a thin little cardboard about five inches long that had tiny red flowers on one side and tiny writing on the other. I frowned up at her. "I don't remember..."

"Just take it," she interrupted. "Maybe I'll see you later. Good-bye."

I watched her walk away. Her message about Sherlock Holmes was easy to understand. It meant that she was putting off her "desperate" trouble by not telling her parents about her lost books. Maybe she'd been going to ask me to help again, but the look on Domingo's face and on Rusty's had put an end to that.

I glanced at the writing on the book-mark. "He who rows a friend to the other side of the river," it said, "arrives there, too. Thank you for trying to help me, Ellen."

Domingo said, "Where'd you meet the corn flake?"

I didn't answer. Instead I said, "Why do you call her that?"

"Because she's corny and flaky," Rusty said. "Why else?"

"I don't think she's corny *or* flaky," I said. "What she is is different and smart."

They didn't answer. They both shrugged. And that's when I decided that while Lish and Domingo were searching the back lot as part of Operation Camera, I'd be busy with Operation Bookbag.

Chapter Twelve

I felt good about my decision. To me Ellen's bookbag was more important than Rusty's cameras. I stared across the table at Rusty and Domingo and knew that I'd get Ellen's bookbag for her if it was at all possible, and as soon as possible. There was just one problem. Operation Camera, according to Domingo, had to be put off for a couple of days. This was Thursday and his mother had him booked for "little brother sitting" through Friday. So Saturday morning was the earliest he could go on the search.

"My cameras will be history," Rusty said.

And Ellen will be in "desperate" trouble, I thought. But I didn't want to go over there alone. So before we left the cafeteria, Domingo and I set up a time to meet on Saturday. Rusty said he'd be watching us with binoculars and he told us to be sure to take the red streamers. And Lish said she'd think about whether she was going to go at all.

Waiting until Saturday morning wasn't going to be easy. Forty hours or more to worry about losing my courage. I thought the hours would really drag, but it didn't work out that way. Things were going on in Shadywood Knolls that pulled my mind away from Operation Bookbag.

That afternoon I walked home from school with Lish and two of her girlfriends. When we reached the walk-in gate, we said good-bye to Lish's friends. They went on and we went through the gate. By the time we got to Woodside Lane, we realized that something unusual was happening. First of all, we'd passed one police car on Greentree Road and now here was another one. And there was Mr. Ugly Crane standing in the center of the road, throwing his arms around and yelling at the policeman.

"Wonder what's going on?" Lish said.

"Let's get closer. Maybe we'll find out."

So we crept close to the police car and looked and listened. But we learned absolutely nothing. Unless you counted that Mr. Crane used a lot of cuss words, that he paid taxes, and that the officer should have been there a lot sooner.

I said good-bye to Lish at her corner and kept going on Woodside. It was a nice street. In the warm sunlight the little patches of grass and the scattered flower beds were as bright as a bouquet of balloons. I was feeling pretty good until Queenie came running up to me.

"Hey, Consuelo!" she shouted. "Hey! D'ya know what's happened?"

"No. What?"

"The robbers! The robbers have been here again! All over the place." She jumped up and down as she spoke, her face almost as red as her hair. "They stole Mrs. Packmore's TV and another computer. And they stole my mother's real good jewels and our new VCR. Wait'll my dad gets back from Chicago. He'll really be mad!"

"Did they steal anything from us?"

"Maybe. I don't know. But the police have been here. They've been all over the place."

Once inside the house, I walked down the hall to the small room in the back that was Grace's office. The door was open. Grace was sitting at her desk staring out the window. I kind of hated to bother her, she seemed so peaceful, but then I saw the frown.

I cleared my throat. "Hi. Is something the matter?"

"Oh, Consuelo," she said as she turned to look at me. "No. Well, yes, of course something's the matter. You probably haven't heard about the burglaries."

"I've heard. Queenie told me. And I saw the police cars."

"Well, then you know most of it. The saddest part for me is that they took my little office safe."

"With all your business stuff?"

Grace smiled. "Actually, I never bothered to keep business stuff in it. What I had there was personal. My wedding ring, my pearls, and all the family pictures." She sighed. "I wish now I'd put them in frames, but it's too late for that."

I thought of my busted locket. "I think I know how you feel," I said.

"Maybe you do," she said, giving me a long look. "In any case, it could have been worse."

"Maybe they'll find it," I said, "and you'll get all your things back." And then, "Are there any of the oatmeal cook... I mean the oatmeal rocks left?" Grace grinned and nodded, and I went into the kitchen to find them.

There was a special meeting of the Shadywood Knolls Council that night. I suppose Mr. Crane complained about the police being so slow and about how his taxes paid their salaries, just as he had that afternoon, but if he did, I didn't hear him. Lish telephoned just as the meeting started and we talked for quite a while.

She said nothing was stolen from her house, and she wondered why they'd been so lucky. When Lish and I were through talking, Rusty called. His dad had discovered that his cameras were missing and was furious. But not at him. That was because his dad figured the burglars had taken them. Rusty ended by saying that things were kind of mixed up, but that he'd figure what to do when—and if—we found the cameras.

At school the next day I saw Ellen before she saw me. I ran an errand to the library for my English teacher, and there was Ellen. She was standing behind the counter, busy as a beaver in a red tee shirt, stamping and sorting books. I should have known. Ellen. Books.

After I'd delivered the note I was carrying to Miss Scott, the librarian, I said goodbye to Ellen. I could tell she wanted to talk to me, but Miss Scott was right beside her, so that was that.

One more interesting thing happened at school that Friday. While I was at my locker after home room, the girl with the mile-long lashes came up to me and said, "You can talk Spanish, can't you?"

"Sure," I said. "Domingo must have told you."

"Uh-uh. I could tell you understood us that day when you moved your tray to another table. My name's Emilia. Come sit with us at lunchtime if you want."

"You mean at the table in the corner?"

When she nodded, I said, "Thanks. That's nice of you. And, I'm called Consuelo."

She shrugged and walked away. After a couple of steps she stopped and turned around. "Don't be like Domingo," she called. "He doesn't know where he belongs."

I wasn't really sure that I knew what she meant by that, so I just waved good-bye. I spent most of the rest of the day—while I walked home from school, at dinner, and even watching TV—trying to figure out a way to get out of the house early Saturday morning without Grace's wondering what I was up to.

The brainwork going on in my head must have shown through because at bedtime Grace said, "You look worn out, honey. Do you feel all right?"

"Sure," I said. "I'm fine."

She put her hand on my forehead just like my mother always had. "No fever," she said. "I'm glad you're okay, but I hope you'll sleep late anyway. I have to show a house tomorrow morning, but I'll be home by noon."

So I had tired my head out for nothing. Grace wouldn't even know where I had been.

At nine, just as we agreed, I met Domingo by the fence boards I'd scratched the x's on. We got there just about the same time but from different directions.

Domingo said, "Hi. All ready for Operation Friendship?"

"Sure," I said. I was glad he hadn't called it Operation Cameras because I didn't want to feel any guiltier.

Before Domingo had squeezed through the opening in the fence—he's bigger than I am and it was a struggle—here came Lish, all pink-faced and panting. "Wait for me! I'm coming, too!"

She followed us through the fence and then pushed the boards into place. So there we were, the three of us, staring at the back side of New York.

Domingo said, "Since we're so near the back of the lot, let's start looking from this end of New York."

❧❧

"Where exactly are you going to look?"
Lish said.

"Anywhere a camera could be hidden."

Lish made a face. "That'll take a long time."

"So we'd better get started," Domingo said.

"Sure," I said. "You guys go ahead. I'll catch up with you in a minute."

"Where you going?" Lish demanded.

"Just over here," I said, and, before she could say anything more, I ran toward the Shadywood end of the New York street. Once there, I turned and waved. I watched while Lish pulled Domingo toward the castle and then I headed for the fort.

Again I stayed close to the fence. When I was in a direct line with the fort, I paused. Doing this was becoming a habit. I kind of grinned—a sick little grin, I'm sure—as I wondered what was going to scare me away this time.

I had dressed carefully. I wanted to melt into the dirty browns and grays of the back lot. So I'd worn a really faded black tee shirt and old jeans. I'd also remembered to bring

my rolled-up crepe-paper streamer. I bent over and picked up a heavy rock that just fit in the palm of my hand. Maybe that was why I wasn't as shaky as the other times.

I took a deep breath and raced across to the familiar log wall of the fort. I listened for a minute and then edged around the lopsided gate. Inside, I tiptoed to the steps that led to the tower. I listened again. Everything was quiet. Too quiet, I thought, and looked up the shadowed wooden steps. Maybe they were sleeping. No, that was silly. Of course, those men didn't *live* here. But they might be showing up any minute. Quickly, I moved to the half-open storeroom door. Again I stopped and listened. Nothing.

With the rock held tightly in my hand, I moved into the storeroom. I waited until my eyes got used to the dark, then I went in the direction Ellen had gone. I went in and around the boxes toward the back of the room. I was about halfway there when I thought I heard a sound, a breathing kind of a sound, coming from my right, and I knew that there was someone there.

The sound was so faint I wasn't really sure I'd heard it. Maybe I'd seen something, or even smelled something. It didn't matter. Someone was there.

I wiped my cold, sweaty hands on my jeans and tightened my hold on the rock. I didn't move. I stayed right there, huddled against a tall wooden box for what seemed an hour. It might have been three minutes. I needed someone—Rebecca—to tell me what to do. Because I had to do something. I couldn't just *stay here* forever. I began moving back to the door about one inch a minute. When I got to the very edge of the box that hid me, I paused and listened. Then I stretched my neck and got my eye just past the end of the box. And what I saw was red, a mound of red creeping close to the floor toward the door. I didn't need to look any more. I stuck my head out.

"Hi, Ellen," I whispered.

The red mound fell flat to the floor. "Oh, dear jewel of heaven," Ellen said in a long rush of breath, "it's you."

Chapter Thirteen

"It's me, all right," I whispered. "So why don't you get up off the floor."

"Sh-h-h," Ellen said as she pushed herself up. "They'll hear us."

"Who'll hear us?"

"The two men. You know, those from the other day."

"They're here?"

"I don't know."

"This is silly," I said. "I haven't heard them, have you?"

"I must admit, I haven't," Ellen said close to my ear. "But they were here yesterday, so once more I came and went without my bookbag."

❧❧❧

"That's what I figured," I said. "All right. I'll help you."

So back we went to the other end of the room. Not only was it darker there, but the empty crates and cartons were bigger and closer together. We had a lot of squeezing to do. Finally, we found the huge box Ellen had climbed up on before.

"You stand guard while I go over," I whispered. "I have longer legs than you. If you hear anything, warn me." Then I pulled myself up on the box and jumped down on the other side.

I heard a scurrying sound. I guessed it was rats. And I had a real thing about rats. I bit my knuckles to keep from screaming. But I couldn't leave here without Ellen's books. I could see the backpack now, pushed against the wall. When I heard a soft, "Mee-ow," I pulled in my breath and relaxed. A cat. The one Lish had seen, I'd bet. And that meant that there were no rats around.

I shoved the books into the bookbag and pushed it on top of the box I'd climbed over. "Ellen," I whispered, "get it. Here it is."

I heard her pull the bookbag to her. And then I heard something else: a series of tiny squeals. They came from behind a bunch of cardboards and empty cans. I looked over them and found Lish's "crazy-quilt" cat. Nuzzling up to her, trying to find just the right place to nurse, were five little kittens. Two were "crazy-quilt" colors like their mother; the others were black and white. The mother cat didn't seem to mind my looking, and I wished I could stay, but I knew better. I hadn't forgotten where I was. I took one last look and climbed back to Ellen.

"There are kittens in there," I whispered. "They're darling."

"Why didn't you bring one?"

"Why didn't I *what?*" I shook my head. For someone so smart, Ellen was pretty dumb. "You can't take a kitten away from its mother. She'd scratch you to death."

"That's interesting," Ellen said.

I said, "Did you hear anything while you waited?"

"Nothing. Did you?"

"You were the one standing guard," I said impatiently.

Then we circled through the boxes and out the storeroom door. Ellen moved as quietly as a ghost, and I tried to as well. As we passed the stairway to the tower, I looked at it with sadness. How I wanted to see that tower. We tiptoed around the outside gate. Ellen pulled in her breath in a loud, little gasp as we almost bumped into Lish and Domingo.

Lish let out a squeal, and Domingo put his hand over her mouth. She pushed it away and whispered, "Consuelo! You sure scared us! Where were you?"

"And where'd you find the corn... where'd you find Ellen?" Domingo asked.

"Tell you later," I whispered. "Did you find the cameras?"

"Not yet,"Domingo whispered back.

"Cameras?" Ellen asked.

I nodded. "Rusty's cameras."

"The storeroom has no cameras," Ellen said firmly. "I have explored it thoroughly."

"All right then," Domingo said, "let's try the tower."

❧❧❧

Now that Domingo and Lish were here, I felt braver. Of course we'd try the tower. I followed Domingo and Lish back through the gate. I thought Ellen would run home now that her bookbag was safely on her back, but when we reached the stairway, she was right there with us.

Domingo took a flashlight from his pocket and ran the beam over the staircase. "Walk at the ends of the steps," he said. "The ends don't creak so much."

The stairs were wide. Probably to get big things up and down them easily. So up we went, two and two. There was a landing at the top about the size of a small room—or a large closet. Right across from the steps was a big door made of heavy wood boards. The door to the tower, I thought, and I felt prickles of excitement climb up my spine.

Domingo flashed the light around, and when he did my shoulders drooped with disappointment At the edge of the large wooden door, just above the doorknob, was a shiny metal square. And in the middle of that hung a lock. A padlock. Sure, the padlock meant that there was no one around, so we could all stop whispering, but it also meant that we couldn't get into the tower.

"They've locked the door," I said sadly.

"Of course," Ellen said. "To keep us out."

Domingo said, "I wonder what they're hiding in there?"

"With that lock, we're not going to get in to find out," Lish said.

Ellen moved close to the door. "Why not? They've done an exceedingly poor job of setting the plate. Look, they didn't even use bolts, just screws."

"That's right," Domingo said. "With a screwdriver, we could be in in a minute."

"But even if we could, should we?" Lish asked. "Wouldn't that be against the law?"

"Like 'breaking and entering?'" Ellen said. "We may be guilty of that already. My parents have said, 'O-lan, the movie lot is private. If you go in there, you will be guilty of breaking and entering.' And, since I like spending time here, I went to the library and studied it, and the result is that I'm not convinced that they are right. I believe this exciting place is what the law calls 'an attractive nuisance.' It's unprotected and entirely unsafe and..."

"Hey, Ellen, you're right!" Domingo said. "And even if you weren't, we're here, aren't we? So let's do it." He dug in his pocket and brought out a little gadget that, unfolded, had all sorts of things: a little knife, a tiny corkscrew and even a small screwdriver.

It didn't take long to remove the plate. Domingo let it hang from the wooden frame and slowly pushed the door open. We all crowded in the narrow doorway, trying to see around Domingo, who took up most of the space.

He ran the flashlight beam over the room. It wasn't much larger than the landing, and it was *dark*. As the light went from place to place, I saw a wooden ladder that went from the floor to a square opening in the ceiling. The tower, of course. Near the door was a rusty TV tray with an empty potato chip bag and dried-up orange peels. But what I stared at was the back wall. Bunched against it were TV's, VCR's and a couple of computers with their keyboards. On top of a fur coat on the floor were piled

silver trays and teapots and two polished wooden boxes that I'd bet held silver knives and forks.

"The robbers!" Lish squealed.

"Not robbers," Ellen corrected. "Burglars. They're the ones who break into houses."

"What difference does it make what they are?" Domingo said. He was wandering around the room looking in, under and in back of everything. "All I know is that the cameras aren't here."

I'd forgotten about the cameras. The minute I'd seen the stuff in this room, I'd been looking for something else. But I'd looked as carefully as Domingo, and there was no office safe.

Chapter Fourteen

"Let's get out of here," Domino said suddenly. "This is no place to be. These guys are honest-to-goodness crooks."

I looked with longing at the ladder and the opening in the ceiling. But there was no way I was going to go up into the tower. Not today. Maybe not ever.

We all huddled on the landing while Domingo put the plate back on the door and pushed the little rod back in place. All of us, that is, except for Ellen. She is smart. She was down by the gate being our lookout. And good thing, too.

❧❧

"Ps-s-st!" she hissed up at us from the bottom of the stairs. "They're coming! We have to hide in the storeroom."

We were lucky that the stairs were wide. We made a mad scramble down them without falling over anyone—and without worrying about noise either. A herd of elephants would have made less noise. But once in the storeroom, except for a lot of hard breathing and the stupid pounding of my heart, all was quiet.

I don't know where the others ended up, but I squeezed behind an empty crate with Ellen. It was too near the open door, but who had time to be choosy. And, just as Ellen said, here came the crooks. Gruff Voice was talking.

"Well, I'm outta here. No matter what old Chezz says, I take my share and go. You wanna stay, you stay."

"Not me," the other man said quickly. "I'm with you, Nick. But I don't wanna move all that stuff in the daytime."

They started up the steps and the man called Nick said, "We'll just take the little stuff. Let Chezz worry about the rest."

❧❧❧

Ellen nudged me. "Who's Chezz? Or did he say Cheese?" she whispered.

"How would I know? Sh-h-h."

I heard the metal sounds of the lock being opened and the bar pushed back. The man called Nick said, "I'm sick and tired of this place. As soon as we're through up here, we'll check the storeroom, and we'll be on our way."

Ellen pulled at my sleeve. "Did you hear that!"

"Of course I heard that. They're coming down here. Lish! Domingo!" I hissed. We had to warn them. If we left them here, the crooks would find them. And I didn't want to think about that. "Lish! Domingo!" I hissed again. There was no answer.

"No use," Ellen said.

"Come on, then. We've got to get help." I crept out into the open, stood up and moved carefully to the storeroom door. By now I knew the way blindfolded. The door to the tower was open and the men were talking. I don't know about Ellen's heart, but mine was back in my throat as we tiptoed by the stairs to the gate. Once outside, I pressed

close to the log wall and pulled the roll of red crepe paper from my pocket. I threw it across the opening toward New York.

It was a lousy throw. It fell only a few yards from us. I was wondering what to do when Ellen moved. She raced to where the roll was and let it out in curves and circles almost to New York. How did she know to do that? I guess she is smart.

When she came back, I motioned her to follow me. At the fence by the tree I said, "If you got up on my shoulders, could you grab that tree branch and climb over into Shady-wood and get help? I'll keep your bookbag."

Ellen turned pale. "No!" she said. "No! I can't do that. I have acrophobia."

"Acro... *what?*"

"Acrophobia."

She wasn't going to do it, I could tell that. Besides, if what she had was conta-gious, I didn't want her on my shoulders.

"All right, all right," I said. "We'll just have to go the long way."

"I'm sorry I'm afraid of heights," she mut-tered almost under her breath.

❧❦❧

I said, "Forget it. Hurry!" and started running close to the fence.

After only a few steps I stopped. I'd heard something. Voices. And one of them was Juan Pablo's.

"Señor!" I called, loud, but not too loud. "Señor, it's Consuelo! Help us!" The voices stopped. "Señor Juan Pablo," I called again, "it's Consuelo! We need help!"

I heard a scraping sound and then the two end poles of an aluminum ladder appeared above the brick fence. The head that popped up above the fence had a bristly shock of red hair and bright blue eyes. It was not Juan Pablo.

"What're you doing over there?" Queenie said.

"Queenie," I said, "call Juan Pablo!"

"What for?"

I forgot to be cautious. I shrieked, "Get Juan Pablo!"

"What do you want him for?" Queenie said calmly.

Behind me Ellen shouted, "To save our lives! To save our lives! We're in extreme danger. Hurry!"

Queenie's face turned white, freckles and all. "All right, all right," she mumbled, and her head vanished below the fence.

Ellen and I raced to hide behind the tobacco shop door.

❧❧

Less than an hour later the whole thing was over. And it all worked out all right. Mostly, anyway. What had happened was that when I heard Juan Pablo on the other side of the fence, he was talking to Mr. Neeland. They already knew that we needed help because Rusty had seen the red streamers and yelled down to his father that we were in real trouble.

The two men were on their way to the back-lot gate when Queenie caught up with them. She told them there'd been a murder. So Mr. Neeland called 911 on his cellular phone. The police got there just as Juan Pablo and Mr. Neeland reached the gate. And they found the crooks before the crooks found Lish and Domingo.

All the time this was happening, Lish and Domingo were in the corner with the

❧❧

cats. And Domingo was allergic to cats. His eyes were running and his nose tickled, and all they could think of was, what if he sneezed? Lish said that when the two crooks came down the stairs and started nosing around the storeroom, Domingo and she were scared stiff. Which was a good thing, she said, because that way neither of them could move a muscle and make a noise. But when they heard the policemen come into the storeroom and capture the criminals, they scrambled over the box so fast that it crashed to the floor. The mother cat screeched and jumped on Domingo's back and Lish's long hair got tangled on a nail on the crate. No one was hurt, except for the box. It was demolished.

During all this, Ellen and I took turns peeking through the crack in the tobacco shop door. I swear we'd been peeking for at least two days when we saw the police take the crooks away. Then we raced over to the fort. Lucky us. We got there just in time to get in on a lecture on trespassing from Rusty's father.

✄✄✄

"Trespassing," Mr. Neeland was saying, "is a misdemeanor. You kids could get into a lot of trouble. Maybe hauled into court." He went on and on.

Juan Pablo nodded seriously as Mr. Neeland scolded us, but there was kind of a twinkle in his dark eyes.

Ellen kept trying to interrupt. Finally, she did. "To my knowledge," she said, "there is not one 'No Trespassing' sign posted around this lot. Isn't that an offense, too?"

Mr. Neeland bent his head to one side. He stared at Ellen. She went right on. "Besides, this place has not been made secure. And it is entirely unsafe for children. I think the film company should be sued for keeping 'an attractive nuisance.'"

Mr. Neeland's mouth dropped open. Then he choked. Then he cleared his throat. "I'll have to give that some careful thought," he said.

He's a lawyer, of course. Well, at least he didn't say anything about "breaking and entering." What he did say was that we should never, *never* have taken the chances we did for a couple of cameras. We had to draw the line, he said, on what we did for our friends. But he didn't look at all angry when he said that.

I guess he was thinking of all that stuff we'd found upstairs.

Chapter Fifteen

Of course I had to tell Grace all about it. Anyway, if I didn't, Mr. Neeland certainly would. The funny thing was that I really wanted to tell her. I knew that what we'd done was pretty dumb—and pretty dangerous. If Grace was going to scold me, I wanted to get it over with.

When she came home at noon, we made tuna sandwiches and ate them at the little table in the kitchen. When we were through, I said, "I've got to tell you something."

She raised her eyebrow. I wish I could do that. I keep practicing. But I guess I didn't inherit her eyebrow-raising gene. "You sound serious," she said. "What is it?"

❧❧❧

"Two things," I said as fast as I could. I didn't want to give myself a chance to change my mind. "I'll start with what happened in the back lot."

"The back lot," she said. "Hm-m-m. I certainly want to hear about that."

I began at the beginning. From the very beginning. The day that Lish and I climbed the tree to get over. I left out a few things, like that I'd torn my jeans and that when I found my locket it was ruined. I *did* tell her where I'd met Ellen and about Ellen's bookbag. When I got to the part about the room where all the stolen things were, I said, "I looked hard, but your safe wasn't there. I'm really sorry."

"I've already heard about that," Grace said. "Mr. Neeland made a quick inventory of the things that were there and brought it to me." She shook her head. "It never occurred to me that you'd go into the movie lot without permission. You must have had a lot of freedom in Dos Palos."

I guess I nodded because she said, "I see. Well, living in a city is different. You may go anywhere in Shadywood on your own, but...

well, we'll talk about that later. Right now, tell me what's the second thing?"

"It's in Shadywood," I said. "Can I go to Rusty's for a barbecue supper? Mr. Neeland invited us. All of us," I added, because Ellen was invited, too. "He says Rusty will want to hear what happened first-hand."

"Of course you may go," Grace said. "That sounds like fun." But there was something in her voice that made me wonder if she meant it.

A couple of hours later when I went to the refrigerator for a cold drink, I think I figured out why she sounded funny. Piled on the second shelf were the makings for a taco dinner: corn tortillas, salsa and shredded chicken. And even a carton of refried beans. My grandmother had planned a special meal for me, and I think she was disappointed that I wouldn't be here.

At four-thirty the phone rang. I could hear the conversation all the way from the office because Grace had on her speaker phone. It was the gateman telling her that some kid was standing there, claiming that she was on her way to our house. "She's got

❧❧❧

her dander up," he said. "She's saying something about an 'infringement of her rights.'"

"That's Ellen," I called, running down the
hall. "Why is he stopping her? I told her to
come here first and then we'd go to Rusty's."

"Ben," Grace said to the guard, "send her
in. She's my granddaughter's guest." Then
she turned to me. "Remember, this is a
guarded community. Next time, we'll give
the gateman her name and he'll let her right
in."

"That's a dumb way to do," I said.
"Besides, what good is it to have a guard
that stops your friends and lets in a bunch
of crooks?" I was sorry I'd said that, but
Grace didn't get mad.

She just stared at me for a minute and
said, "You have a point. The police are working with our council to find out how those
burglars did get in."

The doorbell rang. And there was Ellen
wearing another red shirt over white shorts.
She said she was honored to meet my grandmother, then added, "My parents would like
to meet you by telephone, please, Mrs. Harburton."

Grace said that was very wise and went to the phone.

As soon as Grace had talked to Ellen's parents, we left for Rusty's. When we were outside I said, "Why do you always wear red, Ellen?"

"Because it's a happy color. A very satisfying color that causes good things to happen."

The barbecue at Rusty's was fun. Hot dogs, hamburgers, three kinds of chips, and cold drinks. Domingo and Rusty were especially nice to Ellen. I don't think it was Ellen's red shirt that caused that to happen. Mr. Neeland was nice to all of us. But I think he liked to talk to Ellen best of all. In any case, Rusty's barbecue was great. Especially his mother's fudge brownies.

Before we went home, Rusty said, "Do you guys realize we really caught those crooks? I think we're a good team. Maybe we can help the police find out how the robbers..."

"Burglars," Ellen said.

Rusty shrugged. "How the burglars got in and out of this place so often and so easy.

What I mean is, did you guys hear anything that might be a clue?"

Lish said, "Nothing but a phony scream."

Domingo said, "I didn't hear anything."

"And I didn't either," I said.

"There *was* one thing," Ellen said. "Those two men had a colleague they called something like, Cheese."

"What's a colleague?" Lish asked.

"An associate," Ellen answered. "Like a fellow burglar."

"What do you mean, cheese?" Rusty said. "Like in a sandwich?"

"It sounded like cheese. You figure."

"Well, that's a beginning," Rusty said. "All of you, put on your thinking caps, and Monday we'll make a list of clues." He was being our leader again.

When Rusty's party was over, Lish and I took Ellen to the walk-in gate. Then I went home. And I went there fast. I wanted to tell Grace all about the barbecue.

I called "Grace" from the front hall. No one answered. I went to her office. But when I got there, I didn't go in. Grace was sitting at her desk, just staring out the window again. I waited a minute, then I said, "Grace, are you all right?"

She turned toward me. "Yes, honey, I'm fine."

She didn't look fine. Her eyes were puffy and kind of red. She smiled a weak little smile and added, "I've just been sitting here thinking."

"About the safe? And the stuff you lost?"

"About a lot of things. Yes. That, too." She got up, came to the door and put her arm around my shoulders. "How was the barbecue?"

"It was nice," I said. "It was okay. But I was wondering. Grace, do you think tomorrow we could make tacos with that stuff in the refrigerator?"

Chapter Sixteen

Sunday was a pretty nice day. For one thing, I didn't have to worry about getting into the back lot for anything. Not lockets, or book-bags, or even cameras. And I didn't have to find out what was going on over there either. I *knew*. Of course there was one sad thing. The tower. I suppose that if I couldn't go up in the tower I could live without it—but it was still "an attractive nuisance."

Grace didn't have to work, so that morning she went with me to the swimming pool and watched while I swam. I guessed that everybody slept late here, because I had the pool all to myself. I thought of Dos Palos and the pond, and for a minute I was homesick.

Then, as I popped out of the water at the deep end, I thought of something and grinned. Rebecca was afraid of water. Whenever I was in the water, she never told me what to do, except get out. Then I thought of something else. I hadn't needed her to tell me what to do in the back lot either. I had done all right without her.

In the afternoon Grace and I went to a mall, a huge mall, bigger than the one in Redtree. She bought me a new jacket for school, a pair of jeans and a couple of tee shirts.

"I'd like red ones, Grace," I said, "because red is a very satisfying color." Her eyebrow went up and I grinned at her and said, "Ellen."

Walking out to the parking lot, we passed by the jewelry counter, and I saw the exact locket that I wanted. It was round with tiny little flowers all over it. I stopped for a second and stared at it. But when I saw the price I turned away.

Grace said, "What are you looking at?"

"Nothing. Nothing, really." When we were almost to the car I said, "Grace, are there any jobs I can do to earn money?"

Grace stopped so suddenly that I bumped into her. "Your allowance!" she said. "I've forgotten your allowance. I always mailed it to your aunt... but now... Well, we'll straighten that out as soon as we get home."

The best part of Sunday was when Grace made the tacos, and that was because she let me help. They weren't quite as good as the ones Tía Alma or my mother made (neither were the beans), but they were great anyway. I ate three of them and dripped salsa juice all over my new tee shirt.

Right after supper, though, our happy Sunday sort of fell apart. First of all, homework. I remembered that I had a ton of homework to do because I hadn't done any on Saturday. All I had done on Saturday was wander around the movie lot, help catch a pair of crooks, listen to a lecture on trespassing and go to a party at Rusty's. So I knew I'd have to go upstairs and study.

The second thing was the telephone. The first time it rang, Grace returned to the living room from her office looking worried. She said, "Honey, will you turn off the TV? I need to talk to you about yesterday."

❧❦❧

I flicked off the TV and bit my lip. I knew what was coming. The scolding she hadn't given me yesterday. But I was wrong.

"Tell me, Consuelo," she said, "did you see anyone else in the fort? I mean, other than the two men the police arrested."

I shook my head. "Only Domingo and Lish and Ellen. We even figured out who peeked at me from the tobacco shop. It was Ellen."

My grandmother frowned. "I can't understand it. They've arrested Chess Crane as an accomplice in the robberies."

"Mr. Crane?" I said, and almost choked. "Is Chess his name?"

"Chester," Grace said. "But, except for Mr. Neeland, everyone calls him Chess."

"Even the crooks do!" I cried. "Ellen and I heard them talking. Only Ellen thought they were saying, 'Cheese.'"

"You heard them talk about him?"

I nodded and she said, "Well, then, I guess the police know what they're doing." She stood up. "I'd better make a phone call."

The phone rang a lot for the next couple of hours. I wanted to call Ellen and tell her

❧❧

about 'Cheese'—I figured Rusty and Lish already knew—but the phone kept ringing for my grandmother, so I couldn't. Just before I went to bed, there was an especially long phone call.

A while later when my door opened a crack, I was still awake. I saw a sliver of light from the hall. Then it opened a little more. Grace whispered, "Are you asleep?"

"No," I whispered back. Then I giggled, sat up and said, "No," out loud.

Grace didn't turn on my bedroom light. But I could still see her as she walked to the bed because of the light that came through the window. She looked awful. She sat down beside me and said, "I want you to know how much I enjoyed today. It was a nice day. Too bad it was spoiled by all the phone calls."

"There sure were a lot," I said. "Thank you for the jacket. I love it. And for the tacos. I liked them, too. It was a very nice day."

She smiled and patted my arm. Then she started to get up.

"Grace," I said, "is something wrong?"

She sighed. "Maybe. I'm not sure. I guess it's just one thing after another. First, the burglaries and all the things that were in my safe, and then the phone calls..." Her voice just drifted off, like it was floating out the window. When she spoke again she sounded awfully tired. "It's hard to lose things that are important to you," she said.

"I know," I said. I'd lost things, too. "I wish I could help."

She got up suddenly. "You would if you could, honey. I realize that. Good night." She walked quickly to the door and closed it softly.

I lay looking up at the ceiling for a while. Then I got up and dug in my dresser drawer. I found what I was looking for and tiptoed down the hall to Grace's door. It wasn't closed, so I knocked and pushed it open.

She was in a pretty pink robe, sitting in a big armchair. The book in her lap slid to the floor as she turned toward me. "Consuelo. Come in."

"Am I bothering you?"

"Of course not. I was just sitting here thinking. What do you want, honey?"

❧❧

"I've got something for you. It's probably not as good as what you lost in your safe, but it's the only one I've got." I stopped halfway to her and kept on babbling. "I was saving it for a new locket, but, well, you seemed so sad and..." I was talking too much. I ran up to her. "Here," I said, dropping the picture of my parents on her lap, "this is for you."

I would have swung around and run, but Grace had my hand. She had seen the picture, all right, but right now she wasn't looking at it. She was looking up at me.

"Consuelo," she said, and pulled me close to her. "Consuelo, honey, do you know how much I love you?"

Maybe Rebecca would have said that my grandmother was too old to cry, but I guess I didn't think so. Anyway, I didn't mind. I just went to the dresser and got the box of Kleenex.

Chapter Seventeen

On Monday, two very important letters came for me.

Of course, I didn't know about the letters until I got home from school. At school we were so busy passing notes about Mr. Crane and making up jokes about "Cheese," that I didn't think of Grace, or Dos Palos, or anything else. Certainly not letters.

Rusty was disappointed that we weren't going to collect clues for the police now that they'd caught Mr. Crane. I think he was planning on all of us becoming private eyes. Which would have been exactly right for Ellen, what with Sherlock Holmes and all. I don't know about the others, but I'd had enough of snooping. In dangerous places anyway.

At lunch Domingo said that since there were no cameras to look for and no plans to make, he'd go have lunch with his other buddies, the kids from Arroyo Street.

That reminded me that Mr. Crane had called me an "Arroyo Street kid." I looked over my shoulder to the table in the corner and asked, "Are you guys a gang?"

Domingo shook his head. "Not a gang like on TV. We all live in the same neighborhood. You know, a *barrio*. And we all grew up together, so we hang together."

"Emilia said I could have lunch with you guys if I wanted," I said. "Maybe I will once in a while."

"That's a very eclectic thing to do," Ellen said.

"Eclectic?" I said. "That sounds like a medicine."

"Well, it's not," Ellen answered. "It means to draw from all sources. It's a very good thing to do."

On the way home from school Lish and I tried finding silly definitions for Ellen's big words. Like, "Ravenous means to rave on and on." We finally gave up because we were laughing too hard. I waved good bye to Lish at her corner.

It was a good thing that I'd had a few laughs with Lish because once I got home things turned serious. Grace wasn't home, but there was a note from her on the kitchen table. It said that there were two letters for me on my dresser. It also said that she would be home soon. I hurried up to my room.

The letters were from Tío Fernando and Rebecca. I read Rebecca's first.

"Guess what!" it said. "You're coming home!"

I stopped and closed my eyes. Dos Palos. How far away it seemed. Then I read some more.

"I did it!" Rebecca went on in her big, splashy handwriting. "I talked Mamá and Papá into calling your grandmother and telling her we wanted you back. Papá says one more mouth to feed is nothing, and, besides, he has a new job lined up. I told the kids at school that you'd be back soon."

I thought of Jackie Sue and Ruthie and the deaf boy from the trailer park. It would be good to see them again.

"Monica and the twins are planning a party for you. I have something for you, too. A boy who wants to meet you. I know you say you don't want a boyfriend *boyfriend,* but I think it's time you did."

I don't want a boyfriend at all, I muttered to myself. When I do, I'll find my own. I looked at the letter again.

"Papá is going to call your grandmother this weekend. (I guess the weekend will be over when you get this letter). I'll bet you'll be as excited as anything when you read this. I know I am."

I put Rebecca's letter down and stared out the window for a while. Then I picked up Tío Fernando's. His was in Spanish and filled with fancy language. He said I was like another daughter to him and that he would be proud to have me live with them again. Tía Alma had added a note. *"Nuestra casa es tu casa, chiquita.* Our house is your house, little one." I know she meant it.

⁂

I put the letter down. It was nice to know that they really wanted me.

The front door opened then and Tag bounded up the stairs and into my room. I picked him up and went to the head of the stairs.

"Hi, Grace," I called. "I just got home."

"Did you read your letters?" she said from down below.

"Yes. Do you know what they say?"

"I think so. Your uncle called twice this weekend." She sat down on the bottom step.

I went downstairs and sat beside her. Tag went flying into the kitchen. I sat there for a while. Grace sighed a couple of times. Pretty soon she said, "You'll be happy to be back, I know."

"You mean you're going to let me go?"

"I know how much you've missed them," she said. "I'm not going to stop you."

I should have been as happy as Christmas when she said that. But I wasn't. Not that I was unhappy. I just wasn't anything. It was like I didn't know what to think. But there *was* one thing I knew. I didn't want to make Grace feel bad. Not anymore.

"But I really belong to you, don't I?"

"I like to think that," she said. "But I want you to be where you'll be happy."

"So you're going to let me go? You don't have to, do you?"

"No."

"Good. Because I want to stay. After all, living here is a very eclectic thing to do."

My grandmother raised her eyebrow.

"Besides," I said. "I haven't seen the tower yet."

The End

Also by Ofelia Dumas Latchman

Pepita Talks Twice / Pepita habla dos veces, 1995
The Girl from Playa Blanca, 1995
A Shell for Angela, 1995